I0716746

ONLY A KISS

BREAKING THE RULES
BOOK 1

CADENCE KEYS

Copyright © 2023 by Cadence Keys

All rights reserved.

No part of this book may be reproduced in any form or by any electronic or mechanical means, including information storage and retrieval systems, without written permission from the author, except for the use of brief quotations in a book review.

This book is a work of fiction. Names, characters, places, and incidents are a product of the author's imagination. Locales and public names are sometimes used for atmospheric purposes. Any resemblances to actual people, living or dead, businesses, companies, events, institutions, or locales are entirely coincidental. Any trademarks, service marks, product names, or named features are assumed to be the property of their respective owners and are used only for reference.

Editors: Happily Editing Anns

Cover Design: Cadence Keys

Special Edition Cover: Lily Bear Design Co.

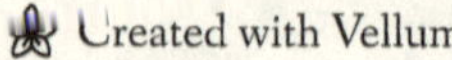 Created with Vellum

For Justin.
You know why ;)

Rule #1

DON'T FANTASIZE ABOUT YOUR BEST FRIEND'S DAD

SADIE

My plush bed supported me as I closed my eyes and fell into the familiar fantasy. I glided my fingers over my collarbone in a feather-light touch. My manicured fingernails traced a line down until they circled the tight buds of my nipples. Nibbling my lip, I pulled them into stiff peaks before pinching hard. A gasp escaped as my pussy clenched, aching for the thick, large cock of the man I hadn't been able to stop thinking about for years. But I needed more than nipple play. I needed to come. Hard.

And only one man had ever been able to get me there. Even if just in my fantasies.

When the boys at school started asking me out relentlessly but would touch me like they were searching for a light switch in the dark, it was *his* voice I'd hear in my head as my own fingers explored my sex and I learned how to pleasure myself.

When I finally lost my virginity at eighteen with my boyfriend who failed to make me orgasm, it was *him* I thought of when I touched myself later until my toes curled and my back arched off the bed as bliss shot down my spine.

When my douchey boyfriend in college was only good for two or three pumps and a truckload of disappointment, it was the thought of *him* whispering dirty words in between eating my pussy like it was his last meal who made my nipples peak into tight buds and my thighs shake as I came.

Every lackluster sexual encounter—and there had been many—had been followed by a solo session and a very particular fantasy of dirty words, sweaty bodies, and an older man who would never see me as anything more than his daughter's best friend.

I let the fantasy come to life in my mind as I moved my fingers away from my nipples and down my stomach, eliciting goose bumps in their wake. My breath quickened the closer they got to the pulsing throb of desire that had been aching for release for hours.

There was one particular moment I usually came back to that never failed to make me wet. A moment I was never supposed to see. A night when Mr. Jones thought Jenna was staying at her mom's house, when instead she'd changed her mind after she got into a fight with her mom. As her best friend, I came over to stay with her because we both thought her dad was going to be out of town.

He wasn't. Something I found out when I got up in the middle of the night to get some water and overheard a moan coming from down the hall. Instead of ignoring it like I knew I should, I tiptoed down the hall toward his room, and my heart beat faster when I noticed the door cracked open. Before I reached the door, another moan rang out, and then a sexy growl that had my thighs clenching and a tingling between my legs that I was still getting used to.

"Yes, baby, take that cock. Fuck. You like how that big, thick cock stretches your pretty little pussy, don't you? Take it all the way. That's a good girl."

My breath stalled completely in my chest at his words and the obscene sounds of wet skin slapping together. I'd never heard him talk this way before—his voice deep, guttural, ragged. He rarely even swore in front of Jenna, so to hear such vulgar words come out of his mouth felt like I was listening to someone else.

But it was the sight that greeted me when I peeked through the small crack in the door that changed my life forever. Mr. Jones looked like a fucking Greek god, his chiseled body glistening in the dim light from his bedside lamp as his hips thrust vigorously inside the pink and swollen pussy lips of the woman draped face down over his bed. I hadn't had sex yet at that point, but that didn't matter.

I wanted to be her.

I wanted to feel his big, fat cock pushing inside my body.

I wanted him to whisper filthy things in my ear and take me to the heaven that he seemed to take her if the euphoric expression on her face—which was tilted in my direction—was any indication.

This time, I imagined I was the woman on the bed from all those years ago. I tipped my head back as my fingers made a circle around my clit, and pleasure built up inside me. This wasn't going to take long.

It never did when I fantasized about *him*.

The one man I could never have, no matter how badly I wanted him. Travis Jones was an upstanding citizen, active community member, a successful business owner, and the man who'd unknowingly had my fantasies in a chokehold since I was seventeen.

I quickened my motion while keeping the pressure light until my stomach tightened and my orgasm ripped through me. But it wasn't enough.

I needed more.

I needed him, but my vibrator would have to do since he wasn't an option. He never would be.

I rolled over and pulled open my nightstand where my favorite cock-shaped vibrator waited. I was already wet from my release, so it slid easily inside me. I turned it on and teased myself, pumping it in and out slowly, like I imagined he would do, his fingers wrapped loosely, but possessively around my throat while he called me his good girl and made my body feel pleasure like I'd never known. My hand quickened the motion of my vibrator pumping in and out of me, each stroke in hitting a place so deep it had me barely able to catch my breath. My stomach tightened once again, the muscles in my legs strained as my body strung tight.

Oh God.

It felt so good.

I kept hitting that spot until my vision blurred and my orgasm exploded through me, ripping out a scream from my throat as my body shook uncontrollably on my bed. Another tremor ripped through me when I pulled the vibrator out quickly, the sensations becoming too much.

I sagged against my bed as my body slowly came back down to earth. The release was exactly what I needed.

And yet...

Like always, I couldn't help but wonder if he'd make it so much better than any fantasy I could come up with.

Unfortunately, even if he saw me as a woman instead of his daughter's best friend who was twenty years younger than he was, I knew he'd never act on it. He'd never sacrifice his reputation in the community, but more than that, he'd never sacrifice his relationship with Jenna.

So, like every time before, he'd remain a fantasy, even if I wished with every breath that he could be so much more.

———

I finished fastening my strappy silver stilettos right as a knock sounded on the door of my apartment.

"Be right there," I called out as I stood in front of my full-length mirror and checked out my appearance one last time. I was running a little late, but I was trying to convince myself that was fine.

Fashionably late was a thing for a reason.

Except that my boss, Shannon, might not agree.

Another knock sounded, and I grabbed my clutch and made my way to the door. Grant Davis stood on the other side looking sexy in a fitted navy suit. If only I could be attracted to him instead. But he was my coworker in a completely platonic capacity. Both of us had been voluntold that we were required to attend the historical society's biggest event of the year—a masquerade ball. Shannon Perry, our boss at Perry Designs, had told everyone that we needed to attend tonight.

I'd been fortunate to get a job at her small firm that marketed itself as a one-stop shop for interior design and eco-friendly architectural design. I'd completed an internship with her my last semester of college, and she hired me on my last day. It was a relief to graduate knowing I already had a job with a very comfortable salary—especially by LA standards.

"Looking gorgeous as ever," Grant said, his crystalline gaze glancing appreciatively down my body. And yet, not a single spark lit up my skin the way it did whenever I saw Mr. Jones. Which was fine, since I suspected Grant wasn't interested in me anyway. He was flirty and friendly with many women, but always held himself back, like he was waiting for someone in particular.

"Got your mask?" he asked.

"Yep," I said, grabbing the silver mask that was resting on the table by my front door. I'd done my makeup with cherry-red lips and a smokey eye that made my blue eyes pop. It was significantly more makeup than I usually wore and had the surprising effect of making me look very different. My long, blonde hair fell in soft waves down my back, and my form-fitting black dress hugged every curve of my body like I'd painted it on. While my mask was currently clutched in my hand, I knew that with it on, I was unrecognizable.

Something that was confirmed when we walked into the venue and found our boss.

"Grant, who's your gorgeous date?"

Grant and I both shared a glance and a smile before I burst out in giddy laughter. Tonight was already more interesting than I had expected it to be, and possibility thrummed in the air.

Tonight, I could be anyone I wanted to be.

The idea made me bolder, more confident, maybe even a little reckless. Especially when I turned around, my glass of champagne halfway to my lips, and my gaze landed on the man I'd been thinking about earlier today.

The man I thought about far too often.

The man who held a mask clutched in his hand instead of covering his face.

Mr. Jones was here.

Rule #2

WEAR YOUR MASK RESPONSIBLY

SADIE

My fantasy in the flesh, he looked mouthwateringly good. He wore a dark suit that was tailored to perfection—hugging his strong biceps and yet still showing off his trim waist. He may have been forty-two years old, but you'd never be able to tell. I wasn't the only woman who noticed him as he made his way down the stairs into the room, his narrow black mask now positioned on his face. He was by himself, and the relief of knowing I wouldn't be tortured seeing him with a woman had my shoulders dropping from where they'd been held stiffly near my ears. I lifted my glass of champagne to my lips and took a hearty sip to quench my suddenly parched throat as I watched Mr. Jones's every movement.

He walked confidently through the room like he owned the place, his shoulders relaxed, one hand tucked casually in his pants pocket, while his other shook hands as he mingled around the tables. He never stayed at one for long, but always made sure to say hello to everyone he knew, and some he obviously didn't.

A smile lifted my cheeks as I watched him network masterfully. The thing was, he wasn't putting on airs like some of the people here. He was genuine in his interest in other people and not just what they could do for him or his business. It was one of the key things that made him such a shining light in the community.

It was also one of the many reasons I'd crushed on him so hard for the last five years.

His steps brought him closer to me, and I held my breath as he approached the table I was standing near. His hazel gaze swept across the table, clearly not recognizing anyone, and then passed by me. He did a double take, and I watched in fascination as his lips tilted up ever so slightly. He walked closer and stretched a hand out.

"I don't believe we've met. I'm Travis."

My heart galloped in my chest. Was he teasing? Or did he genuinely not recognize me?

Testing him, I took his hand, warmth immediately infusing my arm, and said, "I'm Beth."

It wasn't a total lie since Elizabeth was my middle name. I prepared myself for him to lift his mask and make some joke about knowing who I was, but instead he leaned down, his gaze locked on mine as he brushed his lips over the back of my hand.

I sucked in a sharp breath and watched as his eyes seemed to flare ever so slightly.

"Beth. A beautiful name for a beautiful woman."

"Thank you," I said, my voice a breathy whisper. Was he...was he *flirting* with me?

As the reality that he really didn't recognize me started to form in my mind, a new idea popped up, and that feeling of reckless abandon from earlier raised my confidence. How far could I take this?

My heart beat frantically for a whole new reason now. I was about to take a huge risk, one that could potentially blow up in my face if he figured out who I was.

But no risk, no reward, right?

So, I let out a breath and then gave him a seductive smirk of my own. "Aren't you going to ask me to dance?"

A smile lit up his face, and his eyes sparkled even as they smoldered. "A woman who gets right to the point. I like it. Care to dance with me?"

I smiled wider. "I thought you'd never ask."

He let out a laugh and then offered me his hand. I hesitated for only a second before placing mine in his warm palm, trying—and failing—to calm my chaotic heart at the feel of his skin against mine, even if it was something as innocent as holding hands. In all the years I'd spent around him, I'd never touched him. But it wasn't until we glided out onto the dance floor and he pulled me into his arms, our bodies flush against each other as the orchestra transitioned to a slow tune, that all of the years I'd waited for this moment seemed worth it. His firm chest pressed against my lush breasts, and I was sure he could feel my peaked, hard nipples through his tailored black suit. His palm rested against the small of my back, high enough to be appropriate for a first encounter, but I could feel where his pinky rested right near the edge of my ass, and my body *ached* in a way it had never ached before. I ached for him to move his palm lower, to grip my butt like I'd fantasized about a million times. My pussy clenched around nothing as evidence of my arousal soaked my panties. I was on the verge of combustion, and his heated gaze didn't do anything to soothe my aches. His hazel eyes were mesmerizing this close. I'd never truly appreciated the different shades of green that flecked near the iris while the light brown wrapped around it.

My pulse pounded as my gaze dropped to his lips, which were slightly parted as if he couldn't catch his breath. His bottom lip was ever so slightly thicker than his top lip, and I had leaned forward infinitesimally with the desire to nibble at it before I caught myself and moved my gaze back to his eyes. If I hoped I'd find something there that might remind me *not* to act on the impulse I was fighting, I was sorely mistaken. Instead, he looked absolutely ravenous —for me.

He cleared his throat, but it didn't take away from the roughness in his voice when he spoke. "So, Beth. What brought you to this event?"

I tilted my head. "Why do you want to know?" I asked, my voice playful but coy. I couldn't give him too much information or he'd no doubt figure out who I was. I was already nervous enough that if I talked too much, he'd start to wonder if my voice sounded familiar.

His mouth tilted up in a half smirk that made me swoon in his arms. "Well, I'd like to know if I'm going to have an excuse to run into you again, or if I should get your number now."

"You don't know anything about me. It seems a little presumptuous to suggest that you want my number already."

He leaned forward until we were cheek to cheek and his hot breath rushed against my ear. "I know you're the most beautiful woman in this room. I know how you feel pressed against me." As if to accentuate his words, he pulled me even closer until there was no gap between us, and I could feel the developing stiffness between his legs. "I know

I want to know more about you, and I'm a man who goes after what he wants."

Oh God, how I wished that were true, but the second he found out it was me and not *Beth*, he'd never get within five feet of me again.

This could be my one and only chance to see if he lived up to the fantasy. Hell, he could be downright terrible in bed and a disappointment like all the other men in my life. Then maybe I would be released from this unrequited crush that had held me hostage for so long. With a quick glance around to gauge our surroundings, I slid my hand down until I cupped his semi-hard cock. His head snapped back until his gaze locked with mine, and I hoped to God he couldn't see any hint of nerves present. I'd never done anything so bold in my entire life, but I wanted this—him—more than I'd wanted anything, and I wasn't about to miss this chance to finally see if the fantasy compared to real life.

"Prove it," I said, squeezing him just enough that he closed his eyes and let out a soft groan before opening them and staring at me with unrestrained hunger. "Prove you want me."

He grabbed my hand off his thickening member and hauled me out of the room at a speed that almost had me tripping over my high heels. He tried two doors before he came to a third that was unlocked and pulled me inside. The second the door closed, we were immersed in darkness, and any inhibitions I had left evaporated completely.

His hands gripped my cheeks before his lips slammed against mine in a kiss that was full of hunger and untamed desire. I moaned as my hands moved frantically over his suit jacket, eager to get it off him so I could finally feel that toned chest I'd stared at for so many years. He let out another groan that I felt straight in my clit and then slid his hand down my body, squeezing my breast until I let out a sharp cry before diving under my dress and feeling the wet slickness of my underwear.

"Fuck, you kiss like a dream," he groaned right as he shoved his fingers beneath my underwear and then inside me. "And you're so damn wet."

"Oh God," I cried, my legs already trembling as he mastered my pussy like it was his goddamn job. His thumb rubbed enticing circles over my clit while two fingers slid in and out at a torturous pace that was edging me to perfection. My fingers gripped his bicep as I rose higher and higher and then he let loose, shoving his fingers inside me at such a rapid pace it stole the breath from my lungs.

"Travis!"

"Yeah, baby. Give me that orgasm. Come all over my fingers with your hot pussy. Squeeze 'em tight." He moved his mouth right against my ear and whispered, his voice ragged like he was on the verge himself. "Let go, dirty girl."

That was all it took for me to fall off the cliff. I shook uncontrollably in his arms as my orgasm crashed over me in a way I'd never experienced before. I felt completely obliterated and yet somehow, as his fingers slowed and he kissed along my neck and then my lips, I felt whole. Like he broke me with that orgasm and then tenderly put me back together again.

Then he pulled his fingers out of me and put them in his mouth, licking my juices off them. The sound of him sucking me off his fingers weakened my knees, and a new hunger took over.

I dropped to the ground in front of him and undid his belt. He didn't try to stop me. Instead, he pulled my hair into a makeshift ponytail and then held on as I pulled his pants down and gripped his thick, hard cock. He was average length, but very thick, my fingers not even meeting my thumb as I wrapped my hand around it.

I flicked my tongue over the head, and the salty taste of his precum burst on my tongue. My eyes closed in bliss even as my entire body seemed to short-circuit. I wanted to do so much I didn't know where to start, so I followed my gut. I licked from his balls to his tip and was greeted by a deep groan that made my clit tingle. I did it again before swirling my tongue around his head like it was a thick vanilla ice cream cone that I was afraid would drip. Then I filled my mouth with his delicious cock and let out my own moan at how he stretched my lips.

His fingers tightened in my hair a moment before his other hand wrapped around the back of my neck and pulled my head closer. "Fuck, just like that. Suck it down that pretty throat."

His dirty words were going to be my undoing. I wanted more, but didn't think I could handle it. As it was, I was on the edge of combustion. One of my hands gripped his steely length, squeezing and shifting up and down to meet my mouth, while my other hand fondled his balls. I alternated pressures, but it didn't take long to figure out that he liked it best when I sucked hard on his tip while squeezing his cock and jacking him off.

So that's what I did—relentlessly—his words egging me on, until with a guttural groan he released down the back of my throat.

I swallowed it all, my eyes closing in bliss, and already knowing I'd never get over him now.

Rule #3

NEVER SAY NEVER

TRAVIS

My hand gripped my hard cock as I jacked off, but even as I came, I knew it wasn't going to sate the desire that Beth had released in me two nights ago.

She'd dashed out of that closet before I'd even gotten my pants up, and by the time I came out, she was nowhere to be found. And fuck had I tried to find her.

No woman had ever made me feel so weak in the knees as she had—or tasted nearly as good. It had been two days, and I swore I could still taste her. I could still feel the way her tight pussy clamped down on my fingers so hard she could've squeezed them off.

My encounter with Beth had ramped me up in a way no past encounter had. I rarely had one-night stands and couldn't remember the last time I'd done something at all reckless—like fooling around in a closet at a work event.

Probably not since before my daughter was born.

But with Beth, my usual conscience was nowhere to be

found. As soon as my gaze landed on her, she was all I could think about. And not much had changed since she disappeared without a trace. At least Cinderella left a fucking glass slipper. I didn't have a thing apart from her first name, and I had a sneaking suspicion it had been fake since no one at the event knew of any Beths, and no one by that name had been invited.

Regardless, I couldn't stop thinking about my mystery woman, and today was not the time to be distracted. I needed to have my head on straight more than ever.

An hour in my home gym was what I really needed if I couldn't get the sexual release I was craving. By the time I did my last pull-up, my shoulders ached and sweat dripped down my face and back, but I didn't mind. It was the sign of a good workout and fuck, did I need the endorphins after the hell I'd been dealing with at work. The stressors of work were both a blessing and a curse at the moment, but I would've preferred if this week hadn't kicked my ass quite so much.

Nothing had gone right on our latest commercial project. The electrician called me this afternoon to let me know about some additional issues that we hadn't foreseen. Not to mention the new plumber I hired who tried to cut costs by doing shitty work and was only found out because I had suspicions and asked an inspector buddy of mine to check out the property.

We were behind schedule and now over budget due to having to fix the plumber's "cost-cutting" measures. Basically, it was a shit show.

Most days I loved my job as a general contractor. I owned my own business and mostly made my own hours. When I really needed to get out of my head, I could go on a job site and help out with the physical labor. But dealing with this headache and constant paperwork was the one part of my job I didn't enjoy.

I started out in construction, working for a buddy of my uncle's when I was seventeen, and moved to full-time after Vanessa got pregnant with Jenna when we were twenty. Our marriage wasn't a happy one, even from the beginning, but we both felt pressured to try to make it work for Jenna's sake. But I was never the kind of man she wanted, and instead of feeling like a constant disappointment to my wife, I focused on getting my bachelor's degree on nights and weekends. It was stressful for a while, but the money couldn't be beat, especially once I worked myself up the chain of command.

When Jenna was only four, Vanessa and I got divorced, and I was even more determined to build my own business doing what I knew best so I could always be a reliable home for Jenna. I never wanted her to worry about food or shelter. Vanessa caused her enough stress; I refused to add to it. I wanted to be her calm in the storm.

More importantly, I didn't want to fuck up my daughter and have her going to her therapist as an adult about her daddy issues. I was terrified of doing something to mess up, and that was not the dad I wanted to be.

My phone rang, and I grabbed my hand towel, wiping the sweat from my face and then answering when I saw it was Troy, one of my top guys and a good friend to top it off.

"Hey, what's up?"

"Thought you'd like to hear that I'm a genius," he said.

I couldn't stop the grin from forming on my face. "Is that so? I can't wait to hear how you figured that out."

"I can get us back under budget for this project."

"Shut the fuck up."

"I'm dead serious. Your budget was already a bit high

because the cost of materials was rising, but I've got a buddy of mine who works at a wholesale lumber yard, and he can get us the same amount for cheaper. It'll be close, but if my math's right, that should put us right back where we wanted to be."

"If that's true, then I should call your wife and tell her you deserve a big, sloppy blow job because I just beat the hell out of my body trying to figure out how the fuck I was gonna dig us out of this one. I've already blacklisted the plumber. No one decent is going to work with him."

No one fucked with my reputation. I'd worked too hard and too long in this industry for that to happen. My peers respected me, and my community trusted me. No way would I have that tarnished.

Never.

"I don't know how I feel about you having my wife's number, but I'll pass it along that you think she should get on her knees for me."

"I don't, and it's better that it comes from you anyway. Thanks, man. Now I can focus on this bid proposal for the new hotel they're building off Sunset."

"When do you meet with Cline?"

I checked the time on my phone. "Four hours. We're getting drinks at a restaurant in Santa Monica. I should probably get off the phone so I can shower and finalize some numbers for this bid." Cline was a stickler for numbers, and he could be a major cheap ass, but this project would set us up for the rest of the year.

"Go get 'em, Tiger."

I didn't bother saying goodbye as I hung up the phone. Instead, I hustled off to the shower, got dressed in a nice suit —even if I preferred jeans and a T-shirt—and then sat at my desk going over the numbers one more time and filling in any of the blanks based on my latest research and projections. I needed to know this like the back of my hand. Cline might be cheap, but he was smart and very well connected. Everyone knew if he liked your work, he used you for other projects. Even better, he was notorious for having a big mouth, which meant if you got on his good side, he'd sing your praises to everyone he'd ever met, and jobs would come pouring in faster than you could blink.

I'd watched him do business for decades, but I was a nobody back then, just a guy who worked on the job sites.

I wasn't a nobody anymore. I was a self-made man, and it was time to show him that I was the perfect guy for the hotel gig. No one would work harder or be more dedicated to it than I would. No one was more qualified or driven. And absolutely no one would get in the way of me getting this gig and solidifying my name in this business.

The restaurant wasn't busy when I arrived since it wasn't quite the dinner hour yet. The dark wood accents matched well with the beige tablecloths, and the place somehow managed to be both appropriate for business and for a date. The sconces on the table were just slightly more romantic than might be necessary for a business meeting, but the restaurant itself didn't scream romance or elegance. It was cozy and classy.

The hostess greeted me with a flirty smile, even as I kept mine polite but professional. With Beth still on my mind, no other woman ignited a spark of interest. The hostess guided me back to the table where Cline was already seated, a glass with dark amber fluid sitting in front of him.

"Walter Cline," I said, extending my hand. "Travis Jones."

"Ah, Mr. Jones." He glanced down at his watch and raised his eyebrows with a happy little hum. "A man who shows up early. I appreciate that. Time is money, after all."

I smiled confidently. "Couldn't have said it better myself."

I knew how to play the game, even if I didn't always love how fake it felt. Sometimes to win a bid you had to stroke some egos. Cline was brilliant at what he did, and his ego was as big as a skyscraper. I knew walking into this that I was going to be on show. It was exhausting, but a necessary evil.

I reminded myself of all the things I could do with the funds from this project. I could give my guys a much-needed bonus or help Jenna pay for grad school, even though she'd been stubbornly persistent about wanting to do it on her own. This project was my chance to move up to the next tier in my profession.

Which meant it was time to turn on the charm. Cline liked being wined and dined, and talking sports, particularly LA Wolves football. Since I was an avid football fan myself, I had no problem talking sports with him all night. I placed the portfolio with my bid and projections on the table face down and prepared to charm him like he'd never been charmed before.

But before I ever got a chance to speak, the waiter arrived and asked what I'd like to drink. I ordered a Jameson neat and then turned to Cline.

"So, Jones, you're a whiskey man. I like that. I enjoy a fine whiskey myself although I'm drinking a bourbon tonight. I recently went to a distillery and tasted a most unique bourbon blend. Bought several bottles for my collection. Did you know..."

Cline talked about the difference between bourbon, scotch, and whiskey and shared his knowledge of all three for the next hour. I barely got a word in edgewise as I watched his eyes start to glaze with his third glass. My fingers slid across the back of the portfolio, and all my plans slowly disintegrated as I realized he had no intention of going over numbers tonight.

Knowing I needed to stay on his good side, I sipped my drink, then a second, and even a third when he convinced me I *had* to try the one he was drinking. As the alcohol took effect, I relaxed back in my chair, letting my guard down more and more with every moment that passed until my mind wandered to thoughts of bright blue eyes, long blonde hair, and the most luscious lips I'd ever tasted. I had to find that woman again because with every drop of my inhibition from the alcohol, my need for her increased. But nothing could have prepared me for how those low inhibitions would come to haunt me.

Rule #4

KEEP A TWO DRINK LIMIT ON DATES

SADIE

"Another drink, Miss?" The waiter asked me as he tipped the wine bottle toward my glass. My hand immediately shot out to cover the top.

"Uh, no. Thank you." I probably shouldn't have started drinking already since my date wasn't here yet, but I got nervous and thought it might take the edge off.

It didn't.

Of course, some of that might be attributed to the fact my date was now twenty minutes late. I glanced down at my phone, but there was still no response to my text asking if he was on his way.

I reached for my wine glass only to remember that it was empty, which was probably for the best. Glancing around the room, I started people watching, wondering what each person's story was. Were they here with a lover, partner, business associate? Were they celebrating an anniversary or merely going through the motions until the night was over? Were any on a date that started out as disastrously as mine seemed to be?

Then my heart stopped when my gaze landed on the familiar dark hair, square jaw, and broad shoulders of Mr. Jones. A smile spread across his face as he patted another man on the back while shaking his hand. Then they both turned and made their way over toward where I was seated. Shit. He was going to walk right past me on his way to the exit.

I reached for the menu and tried to put it up in front of my face as quickly as possible while curling my shoulders in some lame attempt to hide. But when his warm voice washed over me with recognition, I realized I was thirty seconds too late.

"Sadie?" He stopped while his associate glanced back at him. "You go ahead, Walter. I'll follow up with you tomorrow about that bid."

"Looking forward to it," the man said before he continued on to the exit of the restaurant, and then Travis's piercing hazel gaze focused back on me.

I dropped my menu because it had already failed me anyway, and pasted on a tight smile as I sat up. "Mr. Jones. How nice to see you. What brings you here tonight?"

Seriously, why did he have to look so good? My panties were already soaked just from the way his eyes locked on me with an intensity that left me aching. I still felt the effects of those thick fingers even days later, and the way he looked at me made me wish he knew that I had been the woman he brought to orgasm that night. That I was the woman who sucked on his cock until he came down my throat. I met his gaze, even as my heart swooned a little from being this close to him again.

Why, oh why, couldn't any other guy make me feel even

half as much as I did right then? How was I supposed to stop fantasizing about this man when he had this kind of effect on my body? When I could still remember the sounds he made as he came, or the feel of his fingers gripping my hair?

"Business meeting. What about you?" His gaze dropped over my tight, short, red dress that was riding up my thigh, and my heart nearly stopped at the way his eyes lingered for a split second on my cleavage before they shot back to my face.

Did I imagine that or did he just check me out?

"I'm supposed to be on a date. He's running late." At least I hoped he was running late. I wasn't ready to think about the reality that I'd likely been stood up.

My phone beeped, and Mr. Jones and I both glanced at it to see Josh's name pop up on the screen. I quickly opened the message, and my heart dropped to my stomach as I read his text.

I'm so sorry. I got called into a last-minute surgery. I was trying to ask around to see if someone could switch, but the attending specifically requested me. Rain check?

"Bad news?"

I put my phone face down on the table and fought against my body's natural instinct to slouch in disappointment.

"Looks like he can't make it. He's a doctor and got called into surgery." I didn't know why I was trying to make excuses for Josh. It was our first date. But the idea of Travis judging my obviously poor taste in guys didn't sit well with me.

Not to mention how suddenly pathetic I felt in front of him when this whole night had been a lame attempt to prove I could move on from these ridiculous feelings I had for him. Feelings I knew he could never reciprocate.

He watched me closely with a slight furrow between his brows before moving to the other side of the table and undoing the button on his suit jacket. "Then do you mind if I join you?" He pulled the chair out, but waited for me to respond before actually sitting.

I had to pick up my jaw from the floor as surprise washed over me in waves. My heart started beating faster than a hummingbird's wings as I gestured to the chair. "Please do."

This was completely unexpected, but even more than that, it was anxiety inducing. I knew what we'd done, but he didn't. Already it was hard to keep from squirming in my chair as memories bombarded me with every second that he was in my presence. What if I did something that gave me away?

He sat, and his lips tilted up in the slightest smirk that made me squeeze my thighs together. Fuck, this man was sex embodied. I'd never been turned on so quickly in all my life, and all he'd done was exchange a few words with me and sit down at my table.

Oh, and gave me the best orgasm of my life two nights ago.

The waiter came over and took our drink order, then gave us a few more minutes to decide on our meal. As I perused the menu, I asked, "Did your business meeting go well, Mr. Jones?"

"Travis," he said as he cleared his throat and closed his menu.

My gaze shot up to meet his, and the intensity once again made flutters stir in my belly. "W-what?"

"Please, call me Travis. Mr. Jones makes me feel old, or like my father."

I took a sip of my water to give myself a second to calm down before my voice shook and gave me away. "Okay. Did your meeting go well, Travis?" His name rolled off my tongue like a lover's caress.

I swore his eyes flared and his jaw clenched when his name slipped from my lips; his eyes even seemed to narrow as he watched me more closely. A shiver ran down my spine as I wondered if he recognized my voice from how I'd said his name when his fingers had been buried in my pussy— the way I'd breathed his name against his ear like a prayer as I came undone. Had I already given away too much just by saying his name?

"It did," he said slowly before averting his eyes and shaking his head like he was shaking away an impossible thought. "It was just drinks with an owner I've been trying to work with for years, but the opportunity didn't present itself until now. We're discussing a bid for a future hotel project that could be great for my business. Tonight was a more casual feeling each other out thing, but it still feels like a step in the right direction."

"I'm sure you impressed him."

His mouth tipped up on one side as his eyes lit up. "And what makes you think that?"

I leaned forward and caught his gaze dropping down to my cleavage before shooting back up to my eyes. It happened so quickly I would've missed it if I hadn't been watching him so closely. Excitement pulsed through my body.

"Because you're passionate and brilliant at what you do. He'd be an idiot not to be impressed. No one would be better for a big hotel project than you."

I wasn't even blowing smoke up his ass. I'd never met anyone who worked harder than Travis. I'd always been impressed with his work ethic. How he did it all was beyond me, but it was admirable as hell.

Something in his expression shifted then, like he was seeing me for the first time. And maybe he was. We'd never been alone together—at least not that he knew of—and certainly never talked like this. Maybe it was time for him to see me as something other than his daughter's best friend.

The waiter returned with our drinks, and I eagerly took a large sip of my wine, hoping it would give me the strength to get through this dinner—and not do something monumentally stupid like I wanted to.

"Are you two ready to order?"

Travis looked to me and arched his brow. I nodded, and he gestured for me to proceed. "Steak, medium rare with the potatoes and broccoli. Thank you."

Travis grinned at me, and I felt a blush heat my cheeks as he turned to the waiter. "That sounds perfect. I'll have the same."

When the waiter left, Travis said appreciatively, "A girl who actually eats when she's out instead of simply ordering a salad. That's a novelty."

"I'm a *woman* who knows what she wants. And I like meat."

He cupped his hand over his mouth as he rested his elbow on the table and watched me with amusement and a hint of something else—something that looked like interest, but I was afraid to read too much into it.

I kept my gaze locked on his as I took another sip of my wine. That flutter in my belly flared with excitement when his gaze turned hungry as I put the glass down and slid my tongue along my bottom lip under the pretense of getting any liquid that might've spilled.

He looked down at his lap and cleared his throat. When he looked at me again, he had tempered the heat I'd just witnessed. But it was too late. I saw it and there was no longer any doubt. I hadn't been sure with his other glances, but there was no denying the interest in his eyes only a moment ago, or how he'd once again stoked a fire in my belly that only he could put out.

With his hands.

His mouth.

His cock. God, how I ached to feel that thick cock inside me.

"What are your plans now that you've graduated?" he asked.

I let him off the hook since I was actually enjoying myself on a date for once—even if this wasn't technically a date. "I'm working at the firm where I was an interior design intern. My boss, Shannon, is incredible and really inspirational. When she offered me a full-time position, I didn't even hesitate."

His hand stopped as it held his drink suspended in the air, and his brows furrowed. "Shannon Perry?" he asked. I could practically see the wheels turning in his head as he started to put the puzzle pieces together. Instead of the anxiety I'd felt before at the idea, all I felt was warmth blooming between my legs and a reckless urge to drop more metaphorical bread crumbs until he had no doubt that I was his mystery woman.

He dropped it and tried to move the conversation to Jenna—whether to get us back on familiar territory or remind himself how we were connected, I wasn't sure. But he was too tempting, too sexy, too everything I'd ever dreamed of to stop now. I knew I was playing with fire, but with each sip of my wine, I cared less about the consequences.

"I'm sure you'll miss Jenna when she leaves for grad school. You two have always been attached at the hip," he said.

"Yeah, but we'll get to visit on holidays and whatnot. It won't really be all that different from college." We may have gone to the same school for undergrad, but we were in two completely different programs across campus and only saw each other when we made the effort. We knew how to keep our friendship going even when our schedules didn't support it.

He took a sip of his drink, his eyes never wandering from my face, and I wondered what he saw when he looked at me. "Have you always wanted to be an interior designer?"

I shifted in my chair. That was a deeper question than he probably knew, but I didn't want to drag the conversation down by explaining how I used to design pretty houses and interiors because they were so opposite to the hostility of my own home. If it weren't for my older brother, Daniel, there's no way I would've survived it.

"Pretty much," I said. "I love turning any space into an oasis for the person who's going to use it. I think everyone needs that happy place. And it's rewarding to watch someone's eyes light up with joy when they see the work I've done. I like making people happy."

"I'm sure you do," he murmured, but his eyes sparked with something I was afraid to identify.

For a second we just stared at each other until tension seemed to sizzle between us, and the space between my legs grew damp. I parted my lips on a silent gasp, and his gaze dropped to them before he snapped it back to my eyes, turmoil there, clear as day.

His mouth opened to speak, but before any words came out, the waiter returned with a small basket of complimentary bread. I gave the waiter a smile, even if it felt strained as I tried to rein in the heady feeling of being this close to Travis, alone.

When I glanced at the man in question, he was already staring at me. He cleared his throat. "I'm sure you're as bummed as I am that Jenna's internship goes so long this summer. We'll hardly get any time with her before she needs to go to grad school."

There was something in the slight hesitancy in his voice —like he was desperate to cling to Jenna as a lifeline to avoid what he no doubt felt growing between us—that had me feeling bold. I leaned forward on the table, unintentionally pushing my breasts together, but thrilled nonetheless when his gaze darted down and warmed at the sight before he caught himself.

"I'm not really interested in talking about Jenna right now. I'd rather learn more about you."

His jaw clenched, and he took another sip of his drink, while his gaze locked onto my face like he was determined to figure out my intentions.

"I'm not sure that's a good idea," he said, his voice husky. "I'm pretty boring anyway."

"You're not boring to me."

The corners of his lips quirked up into the semblance of a smile even as his eyes warned me I was teetering on the edge of impropriety. If he only knew how desperate I was to go tumbling over it.

"What do you want to know?"

I answered him honestly, unable to hide how breathy

my voice was at being so close to the object of all my desires. "Everything."

He shook his head, but he smiled like he was flattered, and I loved how the corners of his eyes crinkled and his face lit up when he smiled fully. "You're trying to stroke my ego."

My heart fluttered. His ego wasn't the thing I was aching to stroke.

As if reading my mind, his smile slowly withered until he had that heated look in his eyes again. But it was wiped away just as quickly when our food arrived.

Despite his attempts to keep the conversation innocent, we kept veering into dangerous waters as our conversation naturally shifted from topic to topic throughout dinner.

I'd never spent so much uninterrupted time with him, and it was thrilling to be the center of his attention and learn more about him. He was incredibly smart and insightful, and his intelligence was just as much of a turn-on as his toned physique that he couldn't completely hide underneath his suit. By the time the check arrived, we'd gone through two bottles of wine, and my body was thrumming with need for him—my thighs slick and my panties soaked from my desire.

He watched my mouth while I talked as much as he gazed into my eyes, and the heat that flashed every time he stared at my mouth made me want to be reckless.

Bold.

I wasn't naive. I knew this couldn't really go anywhere. He was Jenna's dad and she would probably hate me if she knew how desperately I wanted him. I couldn't risk my friendship with her, but I also couldn't deny how badly I wanted to push Travis and see how far I could go with this.

Maybe it was the wine talking, or maybe my hormones

were finally getting the best of me. Either way, when he suggested we share an Uber, I didn't object. When he slid in beside me and his thigh rubbed against mine, I didn't move away or even attempt to hide the stuttered breath that escaped at the contact. When the driver pulled up outside my apartment, instead of letting Travis go home like I knew I should, I asked him if he'd walk me up to my door. I lived in a fairly safe neighborhood, but it was still LA.

He stared at me for a long time—until the driver cleared his throat—before his jaw clenched, he nodded once, and then slid out of the car to follow me. As the car pulled away from the curb, we stood only a couple of feet apart, staring at each other as desire thickened the air between us.

I couldn't stop this.

I didn't want to.

I stepped back and he followed as if a string attached him to me—God, how I wished that were true—and he couldn't let me get too far away from him. I spun around and walked up the stairs to my building, and listened as his heavy footsteps followed me up to my apartment until we reached my door. I unlocked it and opened it wide enough to see inside—an invitation—before finally looking back at him. He stood there staring at me, his expression hungry but cautious.

"Thank you for walking me up."

"Sure," he said, his voice deep and ragged and calling to something inside of me that ached for him worse than it ever had.

He took a step closer, although it seemed almost like an unconscious choice. His jaw clenched and his gaze darted around my face like he was looking at me—really looking at me—for the first time.

"Do you need anything else?" he asked.

Only a kiss.

Except truthfully, I knew a kiss would never be enough. I'd had his cum in my mouth and that wasn't even enough. I wanted *him.* All of him.

"Do you want to come inside?" I asked.

He swallowed thickly, his Adam's apple bobbing in his throat before his attention was pulled to something behind me, and I watched with a heady mix of fascination and fear as recognition lit up his eyes. I didn't have to turn around to know what had grabbed his attention, what made him freeze up.

The mask I wore to the masquerade happened to be hanging from my coat rack beside the door.

His attention moved back to me, slowly, but when it finally landed on me it was weighted down by truths neither of us had said out loud. The longer he looked, the more my nipples pebbled sharply against my dress and my core clenched in anticipation.

His gaze darted down to my chest, to the evidence of what his attention was doing to me, and his eyes sharpened with need. He licked his bottom lip before he stepped forward, until his body was only a breath away from mine.

"Sadie,"—his voice was rough and sent shivers down my spine—"were you at the masquerade ball two nights ago?"

I looked into his gorgeous hazel eyes, allowing him to see the truth clearly. "You already know the answer." There was no way to help how breathy my voice came out. It was hard to take a full breath when all I wanted was to feel his lips on mine again.

He groaned and then leaned forward, his hands shooting out to grip the doorframe on either side of me. "Are you..." His jaw clenched again like he was afraid to ask what he wanted to know. "Was it you?" he choked out.

"Yes," I whispered.

He sucked in a sharp breath and closed his eyes as if he was in pain, but he didn't move away from me. Instead, his head dropped slightly, until his nose brushed the hair by my ear, and my eyes closed even as my entire body lit up.

"What are we doing, Sadie?" he asked, his voice husky and sending tingles straight to my clit.

"What do you want to do to me?" I asked, my voice low as my fingers traced along the subtle pattern on his crisp black tie, as I opened my eyes to watch his face.

He shook his head and looked up at the ceiling like he was trying to talk himself out of this. I didn't want him to. I was so close to making my ultimate fantasy come true. And not the one where he ravaged me thinking I was someone else, but where he knew it was me giving him pleasure, making him fall apart with my mouth, my hands, my pussy.

"Travis, do you want me?"

He didn't look at me, but pulled back enough to cover his face with his hand as he let out a strangled groan. He was so close to breaking—I could feel it. So I decided to tip him over the edge he was clinging to.

Stepping closer, closing the little distance between us, I plastered my body against his and placed a kiss on his exposed throat. "Because I want you."

He let out another groan and then gripped my head in his hands and slammed his mouth down on mine. He had me through the door and my back against the wall before I even registered what was happening, but I caught up quickly and rubbed my body against his. My breath stuttered when I felt his hard length between us, and I let out my own moan as he kissed me so passionately it was like he was branding my lips with his.

Rule #5

DEFINITELY DON'T FUCK YOUR BEST FRIEND'S DAD

SADIE

This was better than anything I'd ever dreamed about.

His tongue slid across my lips seeking entrance, and I gave it to him instantly. I'd give him entrance to any part of me he wanted.

My lips were puffy when he pulled away and started kissing down the column of my throat.

"What are we doing?" he asked again in between kisses, and I couldn't tell if he was asking me or himself, but panic filled me to my core that he might stop himself from going further.

"Don't stop," I pleaded, my fingers sliding through his short hair and holding his head to my neck.

"We've had too much to drink." He grabbed my wrists as if to pull them away from his body, but never did. "We aren't thinking clearly," he mumbled before kissing me again.

I was thinking plenty clearly, regardless of the alcohol.

"Please," I begged. "Don't stop." If he stopped, I'd die—

from a combo of disappointment, embarrassment, and lady blue balls.

He let out another groan that was more growl than anything else and swept me up into his arms. "Where's your room?"

"Down the hall. Second door on the right," I said, my voice raspy in a way I'd never heard it before.

He kissed me once more and then carried me through my apartment while I continued to kiss and suck on his neck. The way he squeezed me tighter when I hit a spot he particularly liked only encouraged me further. I wanted him so desperate for me he wouldn't even consider leaving again.

When we got to my room, he put me down, spun me around, and then plastered his front to my back, kissing my neck and shoulder as his hands grazed up and down my sides. My nerve endings felt raw and exposed, sizzling from his touch.

I tilted my head to the side, allowing him more access to my neck, and then let out a sharp gasp when he squeezed my breasts before tweaking my nipples hard. A gush of moisture pooled between my legs, but it wasn't enough. I needed to see him. To feel more of him.

All of him.

Spinning around, I wrapped my arms around his neck, sealing my lips back on his. He met my hunger and stoked the fire even more when he kicked the door shut and then moved me around until my back was pressed against it. His fingers found the hem of my dress and slid underneath until he reached my soaked panties.

He dropped his head to my shoulder and let out another strangled groan. "Fuck, you're so wet." He lifted his head, and his expression turned dominant and fierce but still pulsed with hunger and desire. "You're a naughty girl, Sadie. Tempting me like this."

"Yes," I moaned as his fingers slid up and under the band of my panties. The feel of his skin on mine made me suck in a sharp breath as a jolt of need struck me like a bolt of lightning. My hands clutched his biceps, and when his fingers slid across my clit, I let out another shaky moan, tipped my head back, and closed my eyes at the bliss of his touch.

"Don't stop," I begged again, needier this time.

"Fuck. We shouldn't be doing this."

He moved to pull his hand away, but I gripped his wrist and locked my gaze with his. "Don't you dare fucking stop." I leaned forward, nipping his lip and watching with fascination as his pupils flared with lust. "Make me come, Travis."

I could see the battle clear as day behind his eyes, so I leaned up and nibbled on his earlobe before whispering, "You have no idea how long I've imagined you fucking me blind. I need you to make me come. Please."

"Goddammit," he said before all his restraint snapped. Victory spread through me when he plundered my pussy with his thick fingers, his thumb circling my clit just like he did two nights ago. But this time was so much better because he knew exactly who those fingers were inside of this time.

I gasped and ground down on his fingers as he hit a spot deep inside me that made white spots fill my vision. "Yes, right there."

"That's it. Come on my fingers like a good girl."

I moaned and gave in to the sensations he was coaxing out of my body, the build of my climax feeling bigger than anything I'd ever felt before. Right as it reached the crest, I gripped the back of his neck and pulled his mouth to mine, moaning as our tongues danced and my orgasm hit me full force. My legs shook until the only thing holding me up was his hand still working my pussy into submission.

Holy shit.

It had never felt like this before—raw, needy, perfect. He was my new drug and I was shamelessly addicted. Which was almost comical since I hadn't even gotten the main course yet.

"I want your cock inside me."

He growled, pulling his hand out of my pussy and watching my face hungrily as those fingers of his that were covered with my juices slid into his mouth. "Fuck. Just like I remembered." His eyelids went heavy, and my heart quickened as I watched him lick the taste of me from his fingers.

"You shouldn't taste this good," Travis murmured before he picked me up again and carried me over to the bed where he set me down—gentler than I expected. He pushed the skirt of my dress up until my panties were completely exposed and made quick work of pulling them down my smooth, toned legs. Then he brought them up to his nose and inhaled deeply, closing his eyes like he was in bliss, and whatever breath was in my lungs got sucked out at the erotic image of him sniffing my soaking-wet panties.

When he opened his eyes and focused on me, they were darker than I'd ever seen them, and it was like he'd unleashed a beast inside himself. His hot, hungry gaze seared me to my core, and then without another word, he dropped to his knees, wrapped his arms around my thighs, pulled my ass to the edge of the bed, and then swept his tongue along my slit.

My eyes rolled back for a second before I used whatever energy I could muster to sit up on my elbows and watch him eat me out like I was the gourmet dessert he skipped out on at the restaurant. I'd never witnessed anything more erotic than the way he circled his tongue around my clit until it was plump—his hazel gaze watching my every reaction. My fingers gripped the sheets as he released one thigh to slide two fingers inside me, curling them up as he sucked my clit into his mouth.

I could barely breathe as he watched me while mouth fucking my pussy like a starving man. My stomach trembled as I fought the orgasm brewing because I was nowhere near ready for this delicious torture to end. A whimper escaped as my back bowed, and one hand moved to hold his head against my pussy as my climax hit me. He let out a deep growl that vibrated through my orgasm and blew through my body, wrecking me as I writhed on the bed, my legs clamping his head and my fingers shoved in his hair, pulling on the short strands. Tears streamed out of the corners of my eyes from the power of my release, and I had no doubt my neighbors knew exactly what was happening in here because I couldn't be quiet even if I tried.

Tremors racked my body as Travis kissed my thighs and eased his fingers from my pussy.

"You're so sexy. Too sexy," he said, his voice ragged.

He worked his way up my body, kissing me inch by inch and pulling up my dress until I could sit up enough for him to pull it over my head. I quickly disposed of my bra and then fell back on the bed, staring up at him with complete awe.

No man had ever made me feel like this—completely wrecked and yet more whole than I'd ever known.

I reached up and pulled Travis down until his mouth was on mine, the taste of me still sharp on his tongue. We both groaned as our bodies created friction and stoked the fire between us until I couldn't take it anymore.

"You have too many clothes on," I said.

He pulled back and stood up, stripping out of his clothes but keeping his gaze locked on mine, watching all of my reactions as he exposed his toned body. He didn't have the six pack of a twenty-something gym rat, but he sure as hell didn't have a dad bod either. He'd kept himself fit, and my eyes traced every exposed inch, my body still aching for him even though he'd already made me come twice.

I wanted more.

I was a little worried I would always want more where he was concerned.

He undid his belt, then his pants, then pushed them down past his thighs where they fell to his ankles without any help. His thick cock glistened with precum and my mouth watered. Before I could second-guess myself, I moved to the edge of the bed and slid off until I was on my knees in front of him.

His eyes were molten lava as he stared down at me silently. He brushed away my hair before pulling it into a makeshift ponytail and holding it in one hand. "You want this cock?" he asked in that deep, gruff voice I remembered from our time in that dark closet at the masquerade ball.

"Yes," I said, my voice needy and sex-crazed even to my own ears.

"Fuck, you look so good on your knees. It's even better being able to see you in the light."

My thighs rubbed together in a lame attempt to curb the desire building once again in my core.

"Put it in your mouth like a good girl." He brushed my lips with his cock, and my tongue darted out to taste him. He sucked in a sharp breath and then released a ragged groan when I wrapped my puffy lips around just the head, flicking my tongue on the underside of his cock.

Fuck butterflies—a stampede went through my belly as I got to enjoy every expression that crossed his handsome face while my mouth and hands worked him over in blissful torture.

His fingers gripped my hair. "Oh fuck, yes. Just like that. That's it. Take that cock all the way, dirty girl."

But only another minute passed before he was ripping my mouth off his body and pulling me up for his lips to crash against mine, plundering my mouth until we were both breathless and panting. He quickly grabbed a condom from his wallet and slid it on before leaning his forehead against mine.

"Goddamn, Sadie. What are you doing to me?" His voice sounded broken, and his face was twisted up in plea-sured pain.

I couldn't give him an answer, because in the next breath he wrapped my legs around his waist and guided his thick cock inside my slick pussy.

We both let out a sigh as his hips rocked, pulling his cock out of me before thrusting it back inside until my toes curled. His arms held me tight to his body as he rotated us and dropped me on the bed, his cock still buried deep. He pounded into me with relentless passion until I was a writhing mess on the bed, but there was nowhere to go. Not with his hands gripping my thighs and holding my lower body right at the edge of the bed where he could control the speed and depth of his thrusts. He alternated between teasing me and hitting me so deep, I swore I could feel him in my belly. The thick veins that I'd traced with my tongue glided along my pussy walls like they knew every pleasure spot I possessed. Then he gripped underneath my ass, tilted my hips up, and hit a whole new point that immediately sent my orgasm spiraling through me with complete and utter devastation. My body shook as I screamed, my fingers gripping the sheets beneath me as a way to anchor me to earth—because surely this was what heaven felt like.

His orgasm followed shortly after.

We were both sweaty and panting when he adjusted us so we could lie down on the bed next to each other while we caught our breath.

I also needed to catch reality, but I was worried it was too late for that.

I'd thought our encounter at the masquerade ball had messed with my head, but now I was in so deep, I knew I'd throw caution to the wind for this man.

"You're not at all what I expected," he said, his voice soft and washing over me like a caress.

"You're better than anything I imagined," I admitted on a whisper.

His gaze turned fierce, almost borderline protective, and then he was kissing me again until all I could breathe was him. We lay there for a while, neither of us saying a word as we caught our breath. Whatever excuse we had from the wine had definitely faded, and reality was seeping painfully back into the forefront. There was no excuse for what we had just done.

And there was definitely no excuse for how badly I wanted to do it again.

Rule #6

DON'T ADMIT HOW BADLY YOU FUCKED UP

TRAVIS

I watched Sadie sleep for a long time before I finally forced myself out of her bed. We'd both fallen asleep, but I'd woken up just as the sun started rising and faint light lit up her room. Even as I got dressed, I couldn't seem to keep my eyes off her for longer than a few seconds. She was unlike anyone I'd ever been with before, and I'd been around my fair share of women.

Growing up, my brother, Wyatt, and I were always told we were too good-looking for our own good. There was never a short supply of interested women, and I wasn't going to lie, I was kind of an arrogant little shithead back in the day. But then Vanessa got pregnant with Jenna, and the second I laid eyes on my daughter, I promised I'd never be that guy again. I wanted to be an example of a good, honest man so Jenna would know never to settle for less.

And yet, here I was after twenty-two years of keeping my shit together, staring at Sadie's naked body, barely covered by her dark purple sheets, not feeling good or honest at all.

Except that was only partially true—my body felt better than it had in years, but my head was a goddamn mess of wanting her and knowing I couldn't ever touch her again.

I never should've touched her in the first place.

I'd never looked at Sadie McKay as anything more than Jenna's friend, but last night she seemed completely different. Older. Wiser. I almost didn't even recognize her when I saw her in that restaurant. Maybe it was the absence of my daughter, but seeing Sadie on her own painted her in a new light. I just wish she hadn't been so fucking irresistible—or that I hadn't had so much to drink. Or maybe that I'd never walked her up to her apartment and noticed the mask that had been imprinted in my head since the masquerade ball.

I'd never fucked up this badly.

The one relationship I held above all others was the one I had with my daughter. Guilt weighed down my shoulders as I tried to figure out how the hell things had gotten so twisted up in my life.

I knew I shouldn't have let my goddamn guard down last night. It wasn't Cline I had to worry about—it was this beguiling creature lying naked in bed who blew my fucking mind to blissful smithereens.

Once I was dressed, I sat in the chair she had tucked in the corner of her room facing her bed. I still couldn't force myself to leave. If this was my last chance to look at her like this—peaceful, gorgeous, and completely bared to me—then I was going to soak up every moment.

Once I left this apartment, she had to go back into the box as Jenna's best friend and not the best fuck of my life.

I covered my mouth with my hand as I leaned forward

and rested my elbows on my knees. Why did it have to be Sadie who made me feel like this? Made me feel invincible and needy and such a mess of other emotions I couldn't even separate them all.

I wasn't ready to pretend like last night meant nothing, so I stayed in that chair until my phone started vibrating in my pants pocket. I pulled it out and saw my brother's name flash on the screen. With one more glance at Sadie and her gorgeous, serene face, I reluctantly and silently made my way through her apartment and out of her building, answering the phone once I was out her door.

"Hey Wyatt, what's up?"

My feet felt like lead the farther I got away from Sadie, and I fought my body's desire to turn around and go back to bed with her. To wake her up with my mouth on her pussy until she came and flooded my mouth with her intoxicating flavor.

"Why do you sound so tired? Rough night?"

I scrubbed my face. "It's nothing." The lie sat heavy on my heart. Last night felt like everything, even if it couldn't be anything. "Everything okay with you?"

"Yeah, I just called to see if you wanted to grab some breakfast."

"Sure. Our usual place?" Our dad always took us to the same diner every Sunday for brunch when we were kids. While my brother and I didn't go every Sunday anymore, we still tried to maintain the tradition and go as often as we could.

"See you there in thirty." He hung up without a good-bye, and I pulled up the ride share app on my phone. While I waited, I glanced up at Sadie's building, wondering how long it would take me to recover from last night and how long I could avoid her altogether.

Because despite what I knew I should do and my resolve to do what was right, I was worried that if I saw her again while I could still remember what she tasted like, I wouldn't be able to resist her.

Wyatt showed up five minutes after I arrived, and we both ordered our usual before he leaned back against the booth and draped one arm casually along the back, his discerning gaze watching me carefully.

"Okay, spill."

"Spill what?"

"Don't pull that shit with me. It's my job to read people, so tell me what's going on with you."

Wyatt worked for Carmichael Security—a high-end private security company doing a lot of bodyguard work. He was trained at reading situations and people and acting accordingly, and he was damn good at what he did. There was no way to hide the mess going on in my head. Not from him.

Leaning forward and resting my elbows on the table, I played with an unopened sugar packet as an excuse to avoid his gaze. "I hooked up with a woman last night who's all wrong for me, but it was..." How was I supposed to define perfection? How did I put into words wanting a woman who was so wrong for me but felt so right when our bodies writhed together?

"It was unreal." It was close enough to the truth, at least. "She was incredible."

"Let me get this straight. You're fucked-up this morning

because you had mind-blowing sex last night? Dude, some of us have real problems, you know."

I shook my head, my jaw clenching as I stared out the window. "She's off-limits. I never should've crossed that line and I'm worried if—when—I see her again, I might not be able to control myself, but I cannot under any circumstances go there with her again."

He leaned forward and his eyes narrowed. "Who is it?"

"No one you know," I said, which wasn't at all true. He'd met Sadie plenty of times.

"Bullshit. If it wasn't someone I knew, then you'd tell me."

Our gazes clashed and guilt ate at me. Wyatt noticed it and rubbed his jaw as he watched me. I could practically see the wheels spinning, and dread built in my stomach.

"Someone off-limits...who you will likely see again... Hmm, not many women fit that bill." His gaze sharpened. "In fact, I can only think of one who you would absolutely shit yourself over."

I swallowed thickly, waiting.

"Please tell me it's not who I'm thinking."

"I have no idea who you're thinking." My voice sounded hollow. I hadn't felt this unsteady since Vanessa told me she was pregnant when we'd barely been dating a month.

"Sadie," he said.

I dropped the sugar pack and placed my head in my hands, shoving my fingers through my short hair. The action reminded me of the many times Sadie had done the same thing last night, and I instantly dropped my hands and forced myself to meet my brother's shocked face.

"You can't say a word. To anyone, but especially not to Jenna."

"You actually slept with Sadie?"

"I don't know what happened. It was..." Again, I was at a loss for words. This woman had reduced me to complete stupidity. You'd think I was the twenty-two-year-old in this situation and not the forty-two-year-old.

"We were at the same restaurant, and I stopped at her table to say hi and found out she got stood up. I joined her because she looked so dejected and I couldn't stand to leave her there alone. But instead of it being awkward, she was charismatic, funny, smart. I've never spent any time with her alone—she's always been with Jenna—and it was like she was a completely different person. She's absolutely stunning in every way possible and way too easy to talk to. I'm sure the alcohol didn't help my inhibitions, but if I'm honest, she had me captivated as soon as I sat down. And then once we got to her apartment—it was unlike anything I've ever experienced."

I didn't know why I didn't tell him about the masquerade ball, but it felt like what happened that night—when Sadie and I were just two strangers—deserved to stay between us.

"Are you sure you aren't just making it bigger in your head? I know you've been in a bit of a dry spell."

"It's not because of that," I snapped.

Although he wasn't wrong about the dry spell. I'd always been careful about my sexual partners since Jenna was born, never bringing women home when she was there, except for one time when she was sixteen and I didn't know she'd come to my house after getting in a fight with Vanessa until the next morning. Fortunately, my date for the night had left as soon as we were done, so Jenna never saw her.

Sadie was there that night too, I suddenly remembered. And I couldn't stop my brain from imagining the idea of her watching me that night—even though I know she didn't.

She never acted any differently toward me after that, at least not that I noticed. But maybe I wasn't paying enough attention. She made comments last night in the throes of passion that implied she'd thought of us together a lot—definitely more than just since the ball.

Wyatt's eyebrows formed slashes above his eyes. "You haven't been flirting with her, have you? Like grooming her, because that shit is not okay."

Anger flashed through me. "Fuck you, Wyatt. No, of course I haven't. She was always just Jenna's friend. I never once looked at her like that."

"Not even when she pranced around your backyard in a bikini when Jenna would throw her pool parties."

"No, not even then. What kind of asshole do you think I am?"

"I'm just making sure you're not taking advantage of this girl."

"Taking advantage of her is the last thing I want to do."

"So what do you want?" he asked.

I scrubbed my face and then stared out the window, wondering if she'd woken up yet and how she felt finding me already gone. "I can't have what I want," I admitted, my voice low.

"I'm going to ask again and I want a better answer. What do you want?"

"I want her." It felt good to admit it out loud, even if it wasn't possible, even if I could only say it this one time. Jenna would never be okay with it, and I couldn't lose my daughter. Everything I'd done since she was born had been for Jenna in some way, shape, or form. To better her life and be someone she was proud of. She'd hate me if she knew I had sex with Sadie.

I couldn't even begin to fathom the betrayal she'd feel, from both Sadie and me.

"But you don't think you can have her," Wyatt said, already reading my thoughts. I absently wondered what body language I was giving off that allowed him to read me so openly. I needed to make sure I had corrected it by the time I saw Jenna so I wouldn't be nearly as transparent with her.

"I *can't* have her. She's Jenna's best friend, but apart from that there's also a twenty year age difference. We're too different."

Even if we didn't feel different last night at dinner. Our conversation flowed easily—easier than any date I'd been on in the last few years. In fact, I never once thought about our age difference. I couldn't think about anything but her.

Wyatt watched me closely, his head slightly tipped to the side. Whatever he saw must have stopped him from pushing me to elaborate anymore. "So what are you going to do?"

I rubbed my eyebrow and then looked at him. "Avoid her."

"Seems like the coward's way out. Plus, won't that make things worse? You fuck her and then ghost her like a callous college guy? I expected more from you, brother."

"Then what the fuck should I do?" I asked him, frustrated and pissed at myself because the idea of hurting her felt like a knife to the gut.

"You need to talk to her and at the very least clear the air. If you never want it to happen again, then you need to make that clear. She deserves better than being ignored."

I took a breath, trying to calm myself. "I know you're right, but Wyatt, you don't understand." I leaned forward, my eyes pleading for him to comprehend the minefield he was asking me to walk into. "If I see her again so soon, I don't know if I'm strong enough to resist her. She's *that* addicting."

Wyatt sat back against the booth, and a slight smile lifted the corner of his mouth. "Looks like you need to find that strength or figure out how to have what you want."

I was so fucked.

Rule #7

DON'T FINGER BANG YOUR DAUGHTER'S BEST FRIEND

TRAVIS

Wyatt's advice became a relentless mantra in my mind until I couldn't stand it anymore. So the next day, I went back to Sadie's apartment. I would've preferred to do things over the phone—it was safer for both of us that way—but I didn't have her number and there was no way in hell I was going to ask Jenna for her best friend's phone number.

I could only imagine what a disaster that conversation would be.

Which left me with no other choice than to do this face-to-face, which she deserved, even if it meant facing my greatest temptation again. It didn't help that her apartment only held memories of the way her body felt under mine, the tight clasp of her pussy as she squeezed me until she wrung me dry, the feel of her mouth on my dick, the taste of her pretty pink pussy that was glistening before I even licked her. The whimpers, moans, and screams she made as I fucked her with everything I had.

My cock twitched in my pants as soon as I parked outside her apartment like some fucking Pavlovian response, and I squeezed my eyes closed, giving myself a pep talk about keeping my shit together. I needed to be stronger than this if I was going to survive this interaction— or any future interaction with her for that matter.

I'd mentally prepared myself for seeing her, but as the door swung open, I realized I'd made a fatal flaw. There was no way to prepare for the lust and the memories that slammed into me as soon as she was standing in front of me, her gorgeous blue eyes watching me cautiously, her blonde hair in a messy ponytail, and wearing an oversized sweatshirt that hid the body I'd traced with my tongue.

She leaned against the door in a way that seemed both posed and casual, but her shoulders were high and tight, giving away her tension. Neither of us spoke as our gazes locked on each other, and energy crackled between us until my body felt strung so tight it was on the verge of exploding. The tension grew thick in the air as her eyes turned dark and her gaze hungry.

My heart rate accelerated and my palms grew sweaty as I fought the urge to shove her against the doorframe and ravage her mouth again.

Taste her sweet pussy on my tongue.

Bury myself so deep inside her, it'd be impossible to know where she ended and I began.

She bit her lower lip, and any resolve I had crumbled. We surged forward at the same time, mouths clashing, hands fumbling with clothes as I moved her back inside her apartment and kicked the door closed. She shoved me back against it, her hands pressing on my chest while her tongue glided against mine with a desperation that left me hard and aching for her.

I pulled away just enough to say, "We shouldn't be doing this," before my hand slid in her hair and I pulled her mouth back to mine, kissing her breathless.

In between kisses she said, "I know, but I can't stop."

I kissed her harder as my hand made its way over her breast, squeezing just enough to elicit a moan, before continuing down her body until I slid inside the waistband of her yoga pants, under her panties, and slid my fingers against her slit.

Fuck me, she was soaking already.

"Goddammit, Sadie. What are you doing to me?" What was this fucking power she held over me that turned me into a mindless, needy beast?

"Whatever it is, you're doing it to me too," she said on a breathy moan, grinding her wet pussy against my hand and letting out mewls that made me harder than I thought was possible.

I didn't come here for this—the exact opposite, in fact—but fuck if I could stop. She felt so good, her toned body flush with mine, her lips matching mine kiss for kiss, and her pussy clenching on my fingers like she'd been aching for me. No one had ever made me feel this way—so powerful and wanted—and it was painfully addicting.

With a cry, her body stiffened and then convulsed as her orgasm hit her. I could feel her thighs shake, and I held her tight around her waist, keeping her up against me as I eased my fingers out of her heat.

Her hands came up to hold my face as she kissed me so sweetly, my heart stuttered to a near stop in my chest. It was bad enough we couldn't seem to stop touching each other, but her tenderness made me want so much more than I could ever have with her. Sex was bad enough; a relationship was an entirely different problem.

When she pulled back from the kiss, her dazed eyes focused on mine.

"That's not why I came here," I said.

"I didn't think it was," she said. "But I can't be sorry it happened either."

Collecting myself, I took a step back from her. Space was good.

Space might be the only way I could get through this.

"I came because I thought you deserved a face-to-face conversation. I shouldn't have left yesterday morning the way I did. Not after what happened—what we did."

Her eyes narrowed. "What we did?" I couldn't quite pick up on her tone. It wasn't accusatory, but it wasn't completely composed either. Regardless, it put me on edge.

I rubbed my hand over my jaw, which was a mistake because I could smell her on my fingers, and it made the ache for her worse. I could remember in vivid detail how good she tasted, but I really needed to not be a pervert right now.

"The other night—it shouldn't have happened."

Hurt flashed across her face, but then she lifted her head almost regally and stood tall, confident, and sexy as fuck—although I didn't think that last one was her intention.

"So you came over here to tell me you regret that we had sex, but decided you wanted to finger bang me before discarding me like it meant nothing?"

I opened my mouth to respond, but there was so much to break down from what she said, and I was still reeling from what just happened.

Did I regret that we had sex? No. I regretted that it was a betrayal to my daughter and the faith and trust she'd always put in me, but I couldn't regret the actual act itself.

Especially not when it was the best night of my life. But I definitely couldn't tell Sadie that. It would only hurt her further when I had to follow it up by telling her we could never do it again.

I also didn't decide to "finger bang" her as she so eloquently put it. I swear my brain glitched out whenever I was near her, because I'd never had so little control over my body and my choices as I had with this woman in the last two days.

And I sure as shit didn't ever want her to feel discarded. Fuck that. Sadie deserved to be treated like a goddamn queen. She deserved a man who could proudly walk into a room with her by his side and feel like the luckiest sonofabitch in the world. She deserved a man who could love her in public, instead of only behind closed doors. She deserved the whole world.

I was already jealous as shit of the man who got to be all those things for her. If it wasn't going to risk my relationship with my daughter, I'd volunteer right now on my knees.

But that wasn't our situation, and I had to face reality.

I couldn't have Sadie, no matter how desperately I wished I could. I'd only had her completely once, and I already knew it would never be enough.

Forever wouldn't be enough.

But I couldn't tell her any of that without getting her hopes up. How the fuck was I supposed to do what I needed to do and not crush her?

"I don't regret the other night, but I think we'd be foolish not to acknowledge how complicated that decision has made things."

She still had her guard up, but her shoulders dropped ever so slightly.

"We can't do this, Sadie. Whatever we unleashed the

other night, we need to lock it back up. I can't do this to Jenna."

Her shoulders sagged, and she ran her hand through her ponytail before leaning back against the back of her couch. "I know."

The defeat in her voice gutted me, but I knew this was for the best. What kind of future could we even have?

"I'm sorry. I wish..." She looked up at me and my gut clenched. God, I wished so many things. So many things I didn't ever think about before sitting with her at that restaurant having the best date-non-date of my life.

She nodded like she knew what I couldn't say, but her eyes were sad, and I didn't feel any better than I did before I came here. If anything, I was feeling more confused and fucked-up over the whole thing.

"I understand," she said. "And you're right. I mean, what future could we really have? Jenna would never be okay with this." It was like she was in my head, and it was just another painful reminder of how in sync we were.

"No, she wouldn't. I can't betray her any more than I already have."

"I know," she said so softly I barely heard her. There was a tightness in her voice that made me worried she was going to cry as soon as I left, and I didn't want that for her.

I didn't even want to leave, but I knew I needed to.

I'd said all I came to say. There was no point dragging this out any longer.

"Bye, Sadie."

"Goodbye, Travis."

Without another word, I walked out her door, closing it softly behind me. The sound of it latching echoed in the hollowness of my chest, but I forced myself to keep walking.

Yet with each step away from her, one thought ran through my mind. Why did my dream woman have to be my daughter's best friend?

Rule #8

GET OVER SOMEONE BY HAVING SEX WITH SOMEONE ELSE

SADIE

"What the hell is wrong with you?"

I glanced up at Jenna from my coffee that I'd apparently been staring at for an inordinate amount of time while she filled me in on some vacation her mom was going on with her latest rich boyfriend. She'd called and asked if I wanted to grab coffee and a muffin at our favorite spot after work and I'd immediately said yes to avoid going home.

"What?"

"You've zoned out, like, a dozen times today. What's going on with you?"

I shook my head because what could I actually tell her?

Oh, it's nothing. I just had the best sex of my life with your dad and then he broke my heart in the nicest way—after he finger banged me so hard I saw stars.

Yeah, no.

"It's nothing."

"How long have we known each other?" She arched her brow, and in this moment I hated how well she knew me.

But I hated even more that I couldn't tell her the truth. I'd never lied to Jenna about anything. But I definitely couldn't tell her this. She'd never forgive me.

"Practically our whole lives, but I don't see what that has to do with anything."

"Bullshit. You know exactly what it means. It means I can tell you're not telling me something and it's not nothing. So spill."

I took a fortifying sip of my coffee and then gave her what few details I actually could. "I had a one-night stand and it just kind of fucked with my head is all."

She frowned. "I thought you weren't doing those anymore."

"It wasn't planned," I said.

"Was it bad? Did he hurt you or say something negative to you?"

"No. It's nothing like that." I inhaled deeply, trying to absorb the salty air since we were right near the beach. "In fact, it was hands down the best sex of my entire life."

Her eyes lit up. "Okay, well now I need details."

My heart sprinted in my chest. Normally, I would tell her everything, but this felt supremely wrong to give her details about her dad, even if she didn't know it was her dad.

"It was...there really aren't any words." It wasn't a lie. Travis left me completely speechless after our night together. He brought my body to life in ways I didn't even know were possible.

She shook her head and fake scolded me. "You're no fun for holding out, but I'll let it go this once because I'm more concerned about why it's fucked with your head."

Where did I even begin?

Because I stupidly hoped he'd realize I was the perfect woman for him and profess his undying love for me.

Because when I woke up and he was gone, I burst into tears and then hated myself for crying over a man who never promised me anything.

Because I never imagined Travis would be the love 'em and leave 'em type, and I hated how much it cheapened the otherwise perfect night.

Because when he showed back up at my door with torment written all over his face, I really thought he was there to say fuck it and tell me he wanted to give this a shot.

Instead he voiced what I already knew and then walked out without another word. I was proud of myself for holding it together until the door shut. I wasn't proud of how I'd cried for the last three days and had a broken heart after one night of sex.

"It can't go anywhere, and I'm more disappointed than I thought I'd be because I knew it was only a one-night thing." It seemed like the safest way to sum up my dilemma, even if it left out all the real heartbreak.

"Why can't it go anywhere?" she asked.

"We're too different." It wasn't at all true and the first real lie I'd told her today. I always thought we might be different—due to our age gap at the very least—but that night at the restaurant, I was proven wrong. I was pleasantly surprised to discover we had similar tastes in music, interests in outdoor activities, and clearly we were explosive in the bedroom.

Our compatibility was one of the many reasons it stung so much that we couldn't actually be together.

Her gaze narrowed like she knew I was holding back on her—she probably did—but like a good friend, she could also tell I wasn't ready to go into details. She took a bite of her muffin and then looked at me boldly.

"Well, you know what they say. The best way to get

over someone is to get under someone else. Maybe we should go out tonight and you can find some other guy to rock your world and erase any memory of this guy. I mean, he's clearly a dumbass if he can't see what a catch you are."

I huffed out a small laugh and nibbled the inside of my lip. If she only knew the "dumbass" was her dad.

"I love you, you know that?"

She smiled wide, and it was nice to see. She seemed more herself today than she had since her breakup with Peter. Jenna was in a serious relationship all four years of college. A relationship that ended two weeks ago when, instead of proposing like we all thought Peter would do, he broke up with her. It was a low blow that she'd still been dealing with. "I know. Just like I know you aren't actually going to go out and fuck some other guy. It's not your style."

I glanced down at my cup. "Yeah."

Her smile fell. "He's not worth your tears if he can't see how amazing you are and how lucky he'd be. Don't give him that kind of power over you."

"I know you're right, but that's so much easier said than done." It didn't help that I also wouldn't be able to avoid him forever. His daughter was my best friend in the whole world. I'd spent more time at his house in the past decade than I spent at my own parents'. It was inevitable that I'd have to see him and pretend like nothing happened.

And that was a big part of the problem. How could I pretend nothing happened when I felt like our night together changed everything for me?

"I know," she said. And she did. She knew exactly how hard it was to let go of those complicated, twisty feelings, especially after her own heartbreak.

We finished our coffee and went our separate ways, promising to get mani-pedis this weekend.

Instead of going straight home, I decided to take a detour. When I passed Travis's house, I stopped, parking my car along the curb and staring up at the house I spent so many days in growing up. It looked different now, maybe because I was seeing everything about Travis differently.

I knew I shouldn't get out of the car. I should've driven home, had some wine, and downloaded another dating app to distract me until whatever heartbreak I was feeling disappeared, but I couldn't.

Instead of doing the smart thing, I got out of my car and walked along the narrow walkway that cut through a beautifully manicured lawn and headed straight toward the modern, dark front door. My finger hovered over the doorbell, and my heart raced chaotically in my chest. I pulled my hand back three times before I finally found the courage to press the doorbell.

"What the fuck are you doing?" I mumbled aloud to myself. This might have been the stupidest thing I'd done in a long time, even dumber than having sex with him in the first place.

But then he opened the door and it didn't feel stupid at all. The relief at seeing him—at being this close—was instantaneous. Like coming up for air when you'd been underwater for too long.

"Hi," I said.

His eyes darted between mine, searching for an explanation, but instead of saying anything, he stepped back and opened the door wider.

I walked into the house that was both familiar and suddenly new and spun around when I heard him close the door.

Did I imagine the bags under his eyes or how sad he seemed? Or was he really as affected by all this as I was?

He shoved his hands in his pants pockets. He was wearing suit pants and a white long-sleeved button-down with the sleeves rolled up halfway to his elbows. A tattoo showed on his forearm, and his top two buttons were undone. He looked delicious, and I wished we were different people so I could rip that shirt right off him and devour him right here, showing him that age was just a number and begging him to fuck me.

"Say something," I whispered.

He shook his head, but his gaze stayed locked on mine. "You first," he finally said, almost like it was being ripped from his throat.

I opened my mouth several times, but nothing came out. I didn't really know why I was here, I just knew I couldn't be anywhere else.

Oh God. Had I turned into that clingy girl? Maybe that was why he wasn't saying anything because it was so obvious I was inexperienced and he was probably not used to one-night stands following him home. What if I completely misread the torment I thought I saw on his face?

He must've seen the panic on my face because he pulled his hands out of his pockets and stepped toward me, but on instinct I stepped back.

"I'm so sorry. I shouldn't have come. I don't know what I was thinking."

I moved to pass him, but he extended his arm, blocking my path and placing his hand on my belly. My gaze shot to his at the contact, and I watched his pupils flare.

"Sadie." My name had never sounded more tortured as it did when he said it.

He slid his hand around my hip and pulled me until I was flush with his body. His other hand slid along my neck, and my eyes closed at the contact of skin on skin. I loved the way he touched me. Like I was precious and beautiful and perfect.

Like I was his to do whatever he wanted with.

He had no idea how true that was.

"I don't want to fight this anymore," he said, his voice hoarse. "Even if I know I should."

My eyes snapped open. I could see the turmoil and knew it matched mine. At least if we went down, we'd go down together. I was risking so much by pursuing this, but then again so was he, and clearly neither of us could keep fighting this pull to each other.

"Then don't fight it," I whispered against his lips right before he sealed his over mine and then there were no more words.

Only caresses, moans, and pleasure.

Rule #9

DON'T FALL FOR YOUR "SEX ARRANGEMENT"

SADIE

"Okay, hear me out," I said as I brought the bowl of popcorn back to the couch where Travis was reclining lengthwise in just his boxers. The sight of him lying so casually—and mostly naked—on my couch made a small sigh escape as a giddy happiness bloomed in my belly. I wore his T-shirt and a pair of underwear since his shirt barely covered my ass.

It always seemed so sexy in movies, but I guess I wasn't petite enough for it to work how I thought. Regardless, I felt good wearing his clothes, like it was another piece of him I got to keep, even if only momentarily.

Travis smirked at me as I stood staring at him, my original thoughts completely forgotten and my mind now veering into dangerously naughty territory. It had been a week since that day I came over to his house and we agreed to stop fighting this. *This* had turned into repeated bouts of mind-blowing sex whenever either of us could get a spare moment when Jenna wasn't around, which was often since she was so busy with her internship.

We both said we were just scratching an itch, but with each moment we spent together, I fell deeper and deeper. What had started out as a fantasy had turned into a dream come true—minus the keeping it a secret from my best friend part.

Travis quirked a brow. "You were saying?" He had a knowing smile on his face that made him look so sexy, I had to close my eyes so I could compose my thoughts and get myself back on track.

This was important.

"What I was about to say was why I'm right and you're wrong."

He let out a deep belly laugh that brought a smile to my face. "Oh, I can't wait to hear this one."

My smile grew as I placed the popcorn on the table and then lay on top of him. If I couldn't get him to see sense, then at least I could make him as off-kilter as he made me. His arms wrapped around my back, and I felt him harden underneath me as his smile faded to one of hunger.

"None of that just yet," I said with a quick peck. "I have to school you."

"I can't wait," he murmured, even though his gaze was focused on my mouth and I was worried I was losing him. Better make this quick.

"Christmas is only used as a setting device, but it makes no difference to the story, therefore you cannot categorize *Die Hard* as a Christmas movie."

"I beg to differ. The feeling of Christmas was part of his drive to reunite with his wife and make amends, which drove him to LA, which made it a pivotal plot point to the entire story. And Christmas is supposed to be about family and finding your joy. He got his wife back and killed the bad guys. Family, check. Finding your joy, check." He made little check off gestures with his fingers that had me giggling into his chest.

"You're ridiculous," I said with laughter in my voice as I turned back to the TV where *Love Actually* was playing as part of a Christmas in July marathon. The whole debate about whether or not *Die Hard* was a Christmas movie came up when I asked him what his favorite Christmas movie was.

"We'll have to agree to disagree," he said with laughter in his voice as he brushed my hair back off my shoulder. "I loved watching that movie as a kid. My dad used to rent it all the time. He'd come home from Blockbuster and he'd sit in the recliner while I sat on the couch with him."

"How old were you?" I asked, resting my chin on the back of my hand which was resting on his chest.

He looked at the ceiling. "I think maybe eight or nine. It was just me and my dad since Wyatt was still really little. My mom used to go and read so we could have our 'big guy' time. I remember feeling pretty cool staying up so late watching movies on VHS with him." He looks down at me. "God, VHS wasn't even really a thing anymore by the time you were born, was it? I only remember buying cartoons on DVD by then. I just totally aged myself, didn't I?"

"Maybe a little, but it's cute," I said, able to picture Travis as an adorable little boy who wanted to hang out with his dad. "*Die Hard* still isn't a Christmas movie, though."

"Is that right?" he said with a big grin as he started to tickle me relentlessly until I was squirming and squealing.

"Uncle!" I cried, and he relented, leaving us both breathless, our cheeks flushed and our eyes bright as we looked at each other. But the longer our gazes connected, the more our smiles fell while heat replaced the joy.

I didn't know who moved first, but within a blink our lips crashed together, our hands roaming over skin and our bodies rocking together in a rhythm we'd already perfected. It wasn't long before what few clothes we wore were discarded, and he had flipped us so I was lying with my back on the couch and him hovering over my body.

He started at my neck, kissing the spot where it met my shoulder, and it felt so good, goose bumps spread down my arms. My hands hungrily explored his forearms and biceps as he moved down my body until he reached my nipples.

I'd never been particularly sensitive, and while past boyfriends had loved my full breasts, breast play had never done much for me. It felt good but not great, more like it was another step in the foreplay checkboxes. Where those past boyfriends had never picked up on how little them sucking on my nipples affected me, Travis picked up on it right away. So it didn't surprise me that he didn't spend much time there. If anything, it increased my desire because he was so attuned to my body and what turned me on.

And that in itself was a huge turn-on.

By the time he spread my legs wide to stare down at my pussy, it was already glistening with my desire for him.

"Fuck," he rasped. "This pretty pussy is gonna be my demise."

I lifted my hips, eager for him to put his mouth or fingers or cock where I needed him—I wasn't picky, just needy.

"Look at me," he demanded in that gruff voice of his that only made me wetter. I didn't dare disobey. "That's a good girl. Watch me while I eat this pretty cunt."

"Oh God," I said as my pussy clenched on nothing, aching for him. He dipped down and took a long, salacious lick that had my eyes rolling back until he pulled away. My eyes snapped open to meet his.

"Keep them open and watch."

"Yes, sir," I said with a cheeky smirk that was wiped away with the swipe of his tongue while his piercing hazel eyes held me captive.

His tongue circled my clit before he sucked the tight bud into his mouth, and my legs trembled around his head. His hands gripped my thighs and shoved them down, his eyes sending a clear message.

You'll take all the pleasure I want to give you.

And oh fuck, would I.

My legs shook under his hold as I crested over the wave of my orgasm and crashed back down to earth. Before I'd even come all the way back down, he'd put on a condom and shoved his hard cock inside me and sent me spiraling all over again.

I'd never come back to back before—I thought it was a myth—but there was no doubt this was a new, much more powerful orgasm and not an aftershock of my last one. The ridges of his cock slid along the walls of my pussy like I was made to take him this way, giving us each so much pleasure, it almost felt like too much. My body didn't know what to do with all the sensation as he thrust in and out of me, hitting spots no man had ever found before.

"Travis," I screamed as my stomach tightened with another impending orgasm.

"That's it. Take this fucking cock." He groaned as his hips stuttered. "Fuck, Sadie, you feel like goddamn sin."

My hands slid down to grip his ass and hold him to me as tight as I could, while my insides fluttered and my body felt on the brink of exploding like some kind of supernova.

His pace quickened, and within three thrusts, I tipped

over the precipice I'd been on and took him with me. Both of us were left panting and completely drained, but he was still aware enough to pull me into his arms so we were both on our sides facing each other as he collapsed into the couch cushions.

I let out a blissful sigh and then opened my eyes.

His eyes were closed and his breathing was still a bit labored, but I'd never thought he looked more handsome than he did right then—naked on my couch, a sheen of sweat glistening at his hairline, and his beautiful eyes hidden from me.

He must've sensed me staring because his eyes slowly opened, focusing on me, and there was a heaviness in the air—the same heaviness that was always there after we had mind-blowing sex with each other.

I just hoped he couldn't see in my gaze how hard I was falling for him when that was never part of the deal.

But apparently I wasn't very good at following the rules.

Rule #10

NEVER HAVE SEX OUTSIDE WHERE THE NEIGHBORS CAN HEAR YOU

TRAVIS

My phone beeped with a text from Wyatt, which I promptly ignored as I loosened my tie and pulled up to my house. My heart pounded heavily in my chest when I spotted Sadie's car parked out front. I knew she'd be here—I texted her this morning after I left—but still, seeing her car sent a thrill down my spine that was equal measure excitement and fear. Anyone driving by could see her car.

What if Jenna drove by?

Rationally, I knew Jenna was busy with her internship and not likely to come by for days, but still, the thought that she *could* put me on edge.

Maybe I should've had Sadie park in the garage. Except if Jenna did drive by, it was likely to see me—there'd be no way to hide or explain why Sadie was here.

A bead of sweat pooled at my hairline, and I ripped my tie all the way off and then leaned back against my seat rest. I had to get my shit together.

Sadie and I were just scratching an itch. That was what

we agreed back when she showed up at my house looking vulnerable and so unbelievably sexy I couldn't have denied her even if I wanted to—which I didn't. I wanted her as badly as she seemed to want me.

But we both agreed we were just getting this—whatever the fuck this was—out of our system and then we could move on and never have to mention it to Jenna.

It seemed like a good plan at the time, but the more time I spent with her, the less my desire for her waned. If anything, I wanted her more now than I had the first time. I kept waiting for when I finally felt sated after having her, but my hunger for her was only getting worse.

She was so much more than I ever imagined. Smart, funny, sexy. I'd lost track of the number of times we'd laughed together, both during and after sex. She made me feel alive in a way I didn't know I needed. But I also loved how she had opinions about things and wasn't afraid to share them. We even had a very thorough discussion about the latest international crisis, and I was impressed by the insights she had. I didn't expect it.

Maybe that was my first mistake.

I kept expecting her to act like I imagined other twenty-two-year-old girls did, but she acted more my age than hers.

And goddamn, the sex was off the charts. I'd had my fair share of partners in my life and not a single one held a candle to her. She was a contradiction of bold and submissive, and just thinking about all the ways she owned my body—and even better, let me own hers—had me hard and aching for her already.

"Sadie!" I shouted as I walked into the house and waited for her response. I didn't even let my mind delve into how good it felt to come home to her.

"Back here," her voice came from the backyard.

I couldn't see her until I stepped onto the back patio and then my mouth dropped and my cock hardened even more at the sight before me. Sadie was lounging on one of my pool floats—naked.

I rubbed my hand over my jaw while my eyes ate up every exposed inch of her delectable body.

"I could get used to this," I said, my voice already hoarse from desire.

She smirked, her eyes sparkling. "What are you going to do with me now that you've got me?"

Everything. I wanted to do everything with her. I wanted to taste every inch of her and imprint myself on her the way she'd done to me. I wanted her mind, her body, her laughter. I couldn't have all of that though—at least not permanently—because of who we were to each other, but I could have some of it. I planned to take as much as I could get until my time ran out.

Sitting on the lounge chair, I watched her with hungry eyes. "Come here," I demanded, my voice soft but controlled.

Her eyes never left mine as she slipped off the float smoothly and made her way to me. She walked up the stairs, her body glistening, and my mouth watered. Her steps to me were leisurely, but seductive. The sway of her hips had me clenching my hands into fists at my sides so I wouldn't be tempted to grab her. When she finally stood in front of me, I took off my suit jacket, folded it up, and laid it on the cement in front of me.

"Kneel."

Her eyes flared, but she didn't protest. Instead she got on her knees and looked at me for further instruction. We watched each other while I rolled up my shirt sleeves, and even though no words were exchanged, there was so much said in the silence. The desire between us was practically palpable, the taste of it in the air heavy on my tongue.

I leaned back on my hands. "Undo my pants."

She didn't even hesitate, and fuck if that wasn't an even bigger turn-on. I wasn't a Dominant, but her submission did something to me. Or maybe it was how eager she seemed to be to please me.

She slid down the zipper and then rubbed her hand up and down the rigid length of my cock. My eyelids grew heavy from holding them open when I so badly wanted to close them and relish in how good her touch felt, even over my clothes. Then she slid her tongue along her bottom lip, and I was a complete goner.

"Take it out."

I lifted my hips enough for her to pull my pants and briefs down so she could get better access. She made eye contact with me at the same time her hand gripped my base, tugging up until her thumb slid across the top, rubbing along the precum that had pooled there. I sucked in a breath and didn't miss the way her lips tilted ever so slightly at the corner. She was proud of herself and the reaction she got out of me.

She should've been.

No one had ever made me this fucking needy. Or made me feel so out of control.

I pushed aside her hair and then locked my eyes on hers. "Lick it like a good girl."

Her breath caught, but I knew she loved it when I talked to her like that, and to prove it, she did exactly what I demanded. Her warm tongue glided up my length, from root to tip, as her blue eyes watched my face. My hands gripped the edge of the lounge chair, and my jaw clenched while her tongue circled around my tip, licking up my precum.

"Stop teasing and suck that cock like the dirty girl we both know you are."

Her eyes flared right before she sucked the tip, her cheeks hollowing out and my breath catching in my lungs. God fucking dammit. Her mouth felt so good.

Her eyes sparked in victory at seeing my weakness for her, and then she took my breath away completely when she took my cock all the way to the back of her throat and swallowed. Instantly, my hands shot to her head, holding her in place as my eyes rolled back.

"Fuck yes. Just like that. Choke on that cock, baby."

She swallowed again, gagging a little, and I pulled back, giving her just enough time to breathe before I guided my cock back into her mouth. She let me set the pace, which was good because if she was doing it I would've come too soon. And I was enjoying this way too much to come so quickly.

Her palms slid up and down my thighs before she moved one to gently squeeze my balls while I held her down on my cock, feeling the tightness of her throat. She hummed, and I caught her hand moving between her legs.

"Are you touching yourself?" I growled out.

She hummed again on my cock, her suddenly defiant gaze connecting with mine.

"Show me," I demanded gruffly. "Show me what sucking my cock does to you."

A tremor racked her body, but she didn't deny me as she pulled her hand up and held it close to my face. I let out a groan at the glistening wetness on her fingertips. Just as she went to pull it away, I grabbed her wrist and brought her fingers to my mouth, sucking on them while her pupils dilated and her breath quickened.

Her flavor burst on my tongue, and it was a tease of the juicy goodness between her legs. The taste I couldn't seem to get enough of.

She dropped down and took my cock in her mouth again, focusing solely on the tip. Her tongue slid along the bottom of the head while she sucked, and if she did that too much more, she was going to make me come before I was ready.

She was too fucking good at this.

I tried not to think too hard about who else she'd practiced on because the thought of her with anyone else made me outrageously jealous, and jealousy was not an emotion I was familiar or comfortable with.

I cupped her face and pulled her lips from me with a salacious pop and crashed my lips against hers, sliding my tongue inside her mouth and memorizing every inch. Wrapping a hand around her waist, I pulled her up and flipped us so she was lying back on the lounge chair and I was hovering over her. Then I slid down until my knees were now the ones resting on my jacket on the ground and pushed her legs apart.

It was my turn.

Her pussy glistened with her arousal, and her eyes were deep blue pools of desire as I circled my thumb over her clit and watched her face. I could stare at her all day and never lose interest, which was a terrifying thought because it meant there was a chance I'd never get enough of her.

And then what would I do when I had to give her up?

I couldn't think about that. Not then. Not when she was laid out for me like the most decadent dessert that was made just for me.

I bent down, never breaking eye contact, and flicked my tongue against her clit until she was panting.

"Please," she begged.

"Please what?"

"Make me come."

"Oh, I plan to."

And then I feasted. My tongue dove into her pretty pink pussy, lapping at her juices and letting her flavor explode on my tongue. It was always better straight from the source, but Sadie's flavor was like an elixir from the gods that man was never meant to sample. It was divine and one of a kind.

I moved my mouth to suck on her clit as my tongue flicked against it and slid two fingers inside her, curling up until I hit that fleshy bit of skin that always made her back arch in bliss.

"Yes," she moaned, her hands making their way to my hair and holding my head to her beautiful cunt.

"You taste so good. So perfect. So naughty."

"Travis," she cried my name as I rotated my fingers to hit a particularly sensitive spot I discovered last night. "Don't stop. Don't stop. Oh my god, don't ever stop."

Her body thrashed and shook as her legs clamped against my head and she exploded in my mouth, her cries of pleasure loud, but I wasn't concerned about the neighbors. All I cared about was coaxing every ounce of her orgasm out of her until she was completely spent.

Her thighs still shook around my head, but her death grip subsided and her body sagged against the chair. When I finally sat up after kissing the inside of her thigh, her eyes were closed and a smile lit her face. She was still panting, and watching her beautiful breasts rise and fall while she tried to catch her breath only made me want to watch her come again. I loved watching her fall apart like this.

"You want my cock, naughty girl?"

Her lush lips tipped up at the corners, and her eyes seemed to sparkle as she opened them and nodded her head.

I quickly put on a condom, then lined my cock up at her entrance and in one smooth thrust drove deep inside of her. Both of us let out groans at the same time, her back arched as her hands reached for me, rubbing against my abs. Her pussy fluttered around me with another impending orgasm, and my spine tightened as my own built up to a tipping point. She felt too good. I moved my thumb down to rub gentle circles on her clit, knowing she'd already be sensitive from her last orgasm, and then thrust faster and harder, knowing exactly how she liked it—how I liked it too. She tossed her head back, her eyes closed in rapturous bliss as her pussy clamped down on me so hard I saw stars. My own orgasm hit me like a train, making my legs shake and my heart thunder in my chest—although I wasn't entirely convinced it was the orgasm and not the beautiful woman panting beneath me.

As much as I shouldn't love every second I spent with her, I did. She finally lifted her heavy lids and looked at me with so much tender affection that my heart squeezed painfully in my chest.

I didn't know how I was ever going to give her up.

Rule #11

WHEN IN DOUBT, SAY "NO"

SADIE

"Yes, yes, yes. Right there," I screamed against the pillow as Travis pummeled into me from behind, hitting a spot I didn't know existed inside me.

I never knew pleasure could feel like this or that sex could be this fulfilling. I mean, I suspected, sure, but had no actual proof of it until then, because Travis was a fucking beast in the bedroom. He wrapped his arm around me, his hand landing just under my belly button and then sliding down until his fingers rubbed the most tantalizing circles around my clit. Before I could take another breath, my orgasm slammed into me full force, sucking the breath from my lungs. My body spasmed uncontrollably as I screamed his name.

"Fuckkk," he groaned behind me before his thrusts stuttered to a stop and he released inside of me. I still couldn't get over the feel of him going bare. I'd never realized how much feeling condoms suppressed, but oh my god, it took sex to a whole other level, and I wished we'd had the discussion about going without them sooner.

He collapsed on top of me and then rolled us to the side so he wasn't crushing me. He dropped a kiss to my shoulder and then nuzzled against my neck, and my heart ached with a longing that no amount of sex could satiate. I both loved and hated when he did this. It made me feel treasured, like this could be more than sex.

But reality was not on our side. We'd been having sex every time we could for the past three weeks, but we both knew there was an expiration date on us. His tender affection only made me wish with every ounce of my being that we could be more.

That he could be my everything.

I was a little afraid he already was, which was only going to make the heartbreak more devastating.

Apart from the guilt that ate away at me whenever I saw Jenna, this had been the best three weeks of my life. But every time we finished, there was always a moment where I wondered if this was it. Was this the last time I'd get to feel him holding me skin to skin? Was this the last time I'd hear him say my name while he was buried inside me and making me feel sexier than I'd ever felt?

I wasn't ready for it to be the last time, but I didn't know if I'd ever be ready. I knew without a shadow of a doubt I would be irrevocably hurt no matter when we ended it.

Thinking about the end always made me think about why we had to end it at all, and that guilt slithered its way under my skin again until the idea of facing Jenna made me feel nauseous. How could something feel so right and so wrong at the same time? Betraying my best friend was never something I thought I'd do, but I also couldn't seem to stop myself from craving his touch with every fiber of my being.

"You're addicting," he murmured against my hair, his hand tightening around me and pulling me against him.

"Hmmm, no more addicting than you are."

He huffed a laugh of disbelief, but then kissed my neck and it was just the right amount of tender and sexy to confuse me further.

Was this really just sex for him?

I knew that was our deal, but it hadn't felt like "just sex" ever. He seemed content with our arrangement, but when he held me like this, I started to wonder. Was he as conflicted and torn up about this as I was? Did he crave more with me?

I opened my mouth to ask him, but lost my nerve before any words could escape. I couldn't risk losing him, even if all I got was sex. Which wasn't really fair, because it was more than that whether we admitted it or not. It was dinners together in a prelude to sex, and conversation when we were too spent to move, but not tired enough to actually sleep, and more laughter than I'd ever had with any of my past boyfriends.

It was painful that the best relationship I'd ever had wasn't even a relationship at all, but just a short-term deal.

"What is it?" he asked, his voice quiet.

Of course he could tell something was on my mind. He always seemed to be able to read me, even when I didn't want him to. It was only another reminder of how in sync we were.

"Nothing," I mumbled. I hoped he couldn't tell how in love with him I already was.

He slid his fingers through my hair and then kissed my shoulder. "Tell me."

It was a demand in that sexy voice he used during sex,

and he'd trained me so well not to ignore it. That what would follow his demands was heavenly bliss.

I nibbled on my lip and then closed my eyes as the words escaped my mouth in a mere whisper. "Is this still just sex?" I didn't add the "for you" that was on the tip of my tongue and would give away far too much about how I truly felt, as if this question alone didn't already.

He stiffened subtly, but my body was plastered against his and I could feel it. It was enough to cause my own body to tighten up, waiting for the words I knew were coming.

"That's all it can be." His voice was restrained, but clear.

My heart fell into the gnawing pit in my stomach. It was a confirmation of what I already knew was true, yet it still stung. But of course it was just sex for him. Neither of us were willing to expose the truth to Jenna and risk irrevocable damage to our relationship with her.

"If this is getting too confusing, we can stop." He said it like it was so easy. Like simply stopping was an actual possibility. Maybe for him it was.

That only made my heart hurt more.

Maybe I was a masochist because even as my heart broke, I turned around and kissed him, then told him, "No. Not yet. Soon, but not yet."

He held me to him with a fierce desperation that matched my own. "Soon," he agreed. "But not now."

"Not now," I affirmed again before kissing him, wrapping my leg over his hip and feeling him harden against my belly. For a forty-two-year-old man, I was impressed with his turnaround time.

I rocked against him until we were both panting, holding each other tighter than we ever had. He slid inside me and pulled away from our kiss, watching my face and my every reaction to the way he owned my body.

Our gazes were locked on each other and it felt intimate, but I also felt exposed, vulnerable. Our breaths quickened as he slid in and out at a steady pace, our gazes never leaving the other, our lips only a breath apart. My heart beat at a crazy gallop, and I knew I wasn't doing a good job of hiding my feelings from him—they were plain as day in my eyes and he was watching me like he was staring into my soul.

For the first time since we started this, he didn't speak. He didn't give me demands. He didn't swear. And I didn't either.

We rose to the peak together, our bodies joined in a seductive dance unlike anything we'd ever done before. As we came crashing down together, he finally uttered one single word—my name, said with a mix of bliss, desire, and something else that my love-fogged brain was stupid enough to think could be more than lust, maybe even a love that matched mine.

Rule #12

DON'T LET FEELINGS DEVELOP
WHEN IT'S SUPPOSED TO BE
"JUST SEX"

TRAVIS

My phone mocked me with its silence. I was supposed to be working on putting together a proposal for a potential client, but all I could think about was Sadie.

Her laugh.

Her opinions.

Her body.

Goddamn, her body was heaven on earth. I could get lost in it for days and it still wouldn't be enough. I'd never considered myself insatiable until this woman, but now I couldn't seem to get enough. Every night we spent together only tied me to her more, making me want to know every piece of her, and, even worse, giving her every piece of me. A month ago, she would've never crossed my mind. Now, she was all I could think about. She had completely wrecked me in every way.

I was trying hard not to think about how soon I'd have to give her up because I was nowhere near ready. She mentioned it the other day when we were cuddling in postcoital bliss, and I thought I was going to go out of my skin at the mere mention of us ending things.

The only consolation was that she didn't seem ready to end it either.

But maybe she'd had time to reconsider because normally she texted me back right away. It had been over an hour since I texted her asking if she was coming over tonight.

I pushed aside the new client proposal and moved to the paperwork for Cline. He'd called last week and asked for me to send over an initial bid with my numbers all laid out. We'd gone back and forth a few times with calls, discussing what was negotiable and what wasn't. Our last phone call, he'd mentioned needing a new architect because the original had apparently had a sordid scandal and Cline needed to separate himself from him immediately. The way he spoke about the man made the hairs on the back of my neck rise.

I'd always known what I was doing with Sadie was a scandal in my personal life, but I'd never fully considered the ramifications of how it might affect my business. Would Cline view her as such, or would he just see a man dating a much younger woman as was common in LA?

Why did it even matter if Sadie and I weren't going to last much longer?

My jaw clenched and I checked my phone again, but still no text from Sadie. It was fine. Honestly it was probably for the best. We'd spent every spare moment we could together—a night apart was fine.

When another hour passed without a return text, I caved and called her.

It rang four times and I started to worry it was going to

go to voicemail when she answered, her voice scratchy and hoarse. "Hello?"

"Are you okay?" I asked, concern making me sit up in my chair and lean forward against my desk.

"I'm sick," she said before she broke into a muffled coughing fit. "I'm so sorry. I won't be able to see you tonight." She sounded as disappointed as I felt.

"That's okay. I was worried when I didn't hear from you and wanted to check in."

"What time is it?" she asked as her voice got weaker like she was pulling away the phone to look at the time. "Oh, Travis. I'm so sorry. I fell asleep and didn't even see your text. I..." She broke into another coughing fit. "Sorry," she mumbled.

"You don't need to apologize. I hope you feel better soon."

"Thanks, me too."

She sounded terrible, so I encouraged her to get some rest and then hung up. I spun my phone in my hands, staring absentmindedly at my desk for several minutes before I shut down my laptop, grabbed my keys, and locked the door behind me.

***

"One second," I heard through the door followed by another coughing fit.

When the door finally opened, she looked as bad as she had sounded—and yet she still looked absolutely beautiful. Her nose was red and raw while her eyes were dull and watery. Misery coated every inch of her expression. She was dressed in an oversized sweatshirt that hung loosely on her body and had been cut around the neck to make it looser.

The ensemble was finished with baggy sweats and fluffy socks. She may have been miserable, but she also looked cozy.

I held up the paper bag in my hand from the stop I made on my way here. "I brought you sustenance. I figured you wouldn't be up for cooking."

She leaned against the doorjamb like she was too tired to hold herself up, but her eyes lit up a little. "You brought me food?"

I peeked into the bag. "Chicken soup, Gatorade, cold medicine, and some of your favorite snacks."

When I looked back up at her, her lips were curled up at the corners and her eyes had lost some of her exhaustion. Instead, they were now filled with a softness that made me think she was grateful.

She stepped back and opened the door wider, and I took the unspoken invitation. A blanket was thrown across her couch, and an old romantic comedy from the nineties was playing on her TV with the volume turned low.

"I was trying to see if sleep would knock this cold out, but I can never sleep in the quiet when I'm sick. I always sleep better when I have something playing on the TV in the background, but it has to be something I've seen enough times that I won't feel like I'm missing something if I fall asleep during it. It's weird, I know," she added, as if she was self-conscious of the information she just spewed, but I was fascinated. I loved learning new things about her, and this was definitely something I didn't know.

"It's not weird. Are you hungry?"

She shook her head, but then her stomach grumbled loud enough to wake a hibernating bear and she smiled sheepishly. "Okay, maybe I'm more hungry than I thought."

I smiled at her. "Go sit down and get comfortable. I'll put something together for you."

"Okay," she said softly, her gaze locked on mine. The way she looked at me was a mix between tender and something else. Whatever it was, it made my heart pound heavily in my chest.

She moved to the couch, and I watched her get comfortable under the blanket before I finally pulled my gaze away and moved toward her kitchen. It was mostly clean apart from some dirty dishes in the sink. I quickly got familiar with where she put everything, put most of the groceries away, and then made her a bowl of chicken noodle soup.

I didn't find a serving tray of any kind so I made do with a sheet pan, setting the bowl of soup, some bread, and the Gatorade on it so I could bring everything out to her at one time. I also included a piece of her favorite dark chocolate. I doubted she was up for a lot of sweets while she didn't feel good, but I figured it certainly couldn't hurt.

When she saw the spread, her face lit up. "I can't believe you went to all this trouble."

"It's no trouble at all." If anything, I was more at ease being near her and taking care of her than I was in my office, especially once I heard she was sick. If I was still there, I would've been worried and likely not getting anything done.

No, being here for her was definitely not a burden in the slightest. It felt good to be here for her like this. To take care of her when she needed someone. To be that person for her.

My heart clenched again with an emotion that was becoming clearer by the minute, but I brushed it aside, placed a kiss on her head, and then moved to sit next to her.

A furrow puckered her brow. "What are you doing?"

"I'm sitting on your couch," I said, like it was obvious because I thought it was.

"You're staying?" She seemed surprised, and suddenly I was wondering how shitty her past boyfriends had been that she was shocked I'd stay and take care of her.

But then a different thought hit me. "Do you not want me to?"

"Aren't you worried about getting sick?"

"Not really. If I do, I do. But I'd rather you weren't alone right now."

She stared at me like she didn't know what to do with me. "Okay," she whispered, watching me for a few more seconds before picking up her bowl of soup and turning back to the TV.

We sat in comfortable silence until she'd finished all her food. Then she lay down on the couch and I pulled her feet onto my lap, massaging them gently until she was lulled to sleep. I must've watched her sleep for at least an hour before she woke up, slowly, and then all at once.

As soon as her eyes landed on me, she smiled. And it was so beautiful I almost couldn't stand it.

"You're still here."

"I'm still here." If only she knew how much I was still here.

I'd give her anything I could, except the one thing I knew she deserved—a relationship out in the open—all because Jenna would never accept it. I couldn't break my daughter's heart, and I had no doubt that was exactly what would happen if she found out. She'd hate me, but worst of all, she'd hate Sadie. Then someday down the line—maybe not right away, but eventually—Sadie would come to resent me for what I stole from her, or I'd resent her, which was an equally devastating thought. I couldn't risk it.

The hurt that was coming seemed like a much smarter idea than the hate that could come if I followed my heart.

So even though I'd spent the last hour staring at a woman I could easily see myself with for the rest of my life, I already knew it was a complete impossibility. We were doomed from the start. Because as much time as I'd spent thinking about a future with her, I'd yet to come up with a way to keep Sadie and not lose my daughter.

All I knew for sure was that giving her up was going to wreck me. And no matter what choice I made, someone I loved was going to get hurt.

Rule #13

DON'T LIE TO YOURSELF

SADIE

Every year, the Joneses took a huge camping trip to the lake, and every year since Jenna and I became best friends, I'd gone with them. It was something I looked forward to every summer, but this summer I had a knot in my stomach the size of California. Mainly because I had no idea how the hell I was supposed to be around Jenna and Travis at the same time for three days without her realizing that her dad and I had been fucking like rabbits for the past month—and that I was completely head over heels in love with him.

When Jenna and I arrived, Travis and his brother, Wyatt, had already set up camp. Most of the friends and family that usually came were here, about twenty people in total, and all of them were already more than halfway to drunk if the rowdy laughter was any indication.

"Hey Dad," Jenna said, walking up to Travis who looked sinfully delicious in a pair of jeans that hugged his ass perfectly and a T-shirt that was tight around his chest and biceps, yet loose around his stomach. It didn't help I'd tasted every inch of the rugged body he was hiding underneath those clothes, and my mouth watered at the memory.

"Hey Uncle Wyatt," she said next, pulling my attention away from Travis and the restrained look he sent my way. I glanced over as Jenna hugged Wyatt, only to find him already staring at me with a huge shit-eating grin on his face.

As Jenna pulled away, he said, "Hey Sadie." He walked over and threw his arm around my shoulder, pulling me into a side hug. The uncharacteristic gesture had me glancing up at him at the same time that he shot a sly grin to Travis, and my whole body stiffened.

Did he know?

Did Travis tell him that we'd been having sex?

I tried to covertly glance at Travis to gauge what Wyatt could possibly know when I caught Jenna's confused expression as her gaze lingered on her uncle's arm wrapped around my shoulders. "Wyatt, what the hell? Let Sadie go; she's way too young for you anyway."

Her words hit me like a sledgehammer. My breath left my body in a silent whoosh, and I glanced over at Travis in time to see his face go white as a sheet.

Shit.

Wyatt was four years younger than Travis, so if she thought he was too old for me, father or not, she'd definitely think Travis was too old for me.

Except...he didn't feel old.

When we were together, it felt right. It felt better than any relationship I'd ever been in. I'd never been so completely satisfied, and more than that, he fit every criteria Jenna had always said I should want in a relationship.

Great sex? Check.

Stimulating conversation? Check.

Similar humor? Check.

And now, watching his face, I was terrified that Jenna's offhanded comment was going to destroy whatever bliss we'd had.

Fortunately, Jenna couldn't see the devastation on my face, because she was still focused on Wyatt with her brow arched as she waited impatiently for him to remove his arm from my shoulders. But apparently he hesitated too long.

"That's enough," Travis's voice boomed, catching us all off guard. He cleared his throat. "Leave Sadie alone, Wyatt. She's just here for a weekend away with her friend, not to be harassed by you."

Wyatt winked at him as he lifted his arm away from me. "Whatever you say, Daddy."

Travis glared at him until Wyatt held his hands up in an innocent gesture and let out a laugh. "Alright, alright. I'll stop. No need to be so uptight. You'd think you haven't been getting laid with how much of a stick-in-the-mud you're being."

If I'd had any doubts before about whether or not Wyatt knew about Travis and me hooking up, that one comment squashed them. I knew he wasn't having sex with anyone else—he wouldn't have the time with how much we spent together.

Jenna's gaze snapped to her dad. "You're seeing someone?"

"No. It's nothing," he said automatically. "It was a fling." The last word came out slower like he'd just realized who was present while he denied our importance to each other.

Me.

I tried not to let his words hurt because there was

nothing about them that was news to me. But that didn't make them sting any less or make it any easier to keep breathing and pretending like my heart wasn't shriveling up in my chest.

Jenna frowned. "You know you deserve more than that, right? I know Mom put you through a lot, but you deserve to find a woman who actually loves you and respects you."

He smiled at her and then pulled her into a hug. "Thanks, kiddo."

He glanced up at me while his arms were still wrapped around her, and I fought to keep my face neutral, to not show him how hard this was for me. He made it look so easy.

But of course it was easy for him. He wasn't in love with me.

That sharp pain in my chest expanded. I knew what I was getting into when we started this. I always knew I'd develop feelings; I hated that I was the only one.

I moved back to the car and started unloading our stuff, not as excited about this weekend as I'd been in the past.

"He's having a hard time with this," Wyatt whispered as he joined me at the back of Jenna's SUV while she was still over talking to her dad. "Jenna's been his whole world since the kid was born. He's always put her first."

I knew all of this already. "It's okay. He's right. It is just a fling, so there's no point thinking about it further." I was proud of myself for how easily the words slipped off my tongue—even if it was all a lie.

Wyatt frowned at me, but I didn't give him a chance to say anything more and moved toward where we always set up our tent. Maybe I needed to start taking my own advice and treat this like a fling, or at least take the emotion out of it. I didn't think I was capable of that at this point, but it was worth a shot.

Hell, it was probably the only way I'd make it through this weekend.

Footsteps followed me, and I glanced back to see Wyatt walking over with one of Jenna's bags.

"I could've gotten that," I said.

He looked over to where Jenna was still talking to her dad, but Travis's gaze was locked on us. Then Wyatt turned back to me and lowered his voice. "He didn't mean it, Sadie."

I could pretend I didn't know what he was talking about, but that felt immature, so instead I let out a heavy sigh and focused on pulling our tent out of the bag.

"That didn't make it any easier to hear. And it wasn't entirely a lie. It is a fling, one he obviously told you all about." I shot a look at him and he shrugged.

"He told me less than you might think, but I'm observant. I also usually get him to come to brunch with me on Sundays when I'm not busy with work, but he's been surprisingly busy the past few weekends."

My cheeks heated, but I stayed focused on my task.

"Sadie." The seriousness in his voice pulled my attention away from what I was doing, and I glanced up to see him staring me down, his gaze so like his brother's but much more intense. "Whatever lies you're telling each other are none of my business, but I know my brother, and this isn't a fling for him. Not even close."

But it had to be, or else that meant he was forced to choose between me and Jenna, and that was really no choice at all. His daughter had always been his number one priority. Wyatt knew it as well as I did.

Whether we were lying to ourselves or not, I was going

to be the casualty in this, and maybe that should've made it easier to walk away from him, but it didn't.

Nothing about this was easy.

And that knot in my stomach made me think things were about to get even more complicated.

Rule #14

DON'T PUT YOUR GODDAMN FOOT IN YOUR MOUTH

TRAVIS

I watched Sadie talk to Wyatt and fought against the desire to stomp over there and stake my claim. He was there under the pretense of helping her unload the vehicle while I'd roped Jenna into helping me get the food stuff all organized for dinner tonight. The rest of the group went down to the lake, and we would head down there shortly. But right then, I was hyperfocused on keeping one eye on my meddling brother and the other eye on my daughter so she didn't notice how fucking torn up I was about denying how much Sadie meant to me right in front of her.

Sadie kept her chin held high, and anyone else might not have noticed the subtleties of her features, but I'd made it a point to learn every nuanced expression in the last month that we'd been seeing each other, and I saw the devastation in her eyes.

I saw the way my words hit her like a slap to the face, and now my gut ached and twisted like someone ripped out my insides and made me watch as they stomped on them.

She was so much more than a fling, but Jenna's reaction to Wyatt joking around only made me even more paranoid about her picking up on the chemistry Sadie and I had.

My gaze wandered back to the object of my desires only to catch her tip her head back and laugh loudly at something Wyatt said. He chuckled as well, and my gut clenched as fire roared to life in my body. I'd never once been envious of my brother, but right now, I was. The fact he could laugh and joke so freely with her when it should've been me made me see green.

But I'd always been the responsible one. If I changed my MO, Jenna would think it was weird and then she might question why I couldn't fucking stop staring at her best friend.

Goddamn, I needed a drink.

"Wyatt. Get your ass over here and help me with this," I yelled at him. I needed him to get the fuck away from Sadie so I could tamp down this jealous rage brewing inside me and get my shit together. If I lost it now, there was no way I'd survive the next three days.

He came sauntering over with a smile on his face and said something that made Jenna laugh as she passed him on her way to help Sadie finish setting up their tent.

"Are you pleased with yourself?" I murmured low so no one else would overhear.

"Oh definitely. It's my job in life to rile you up, brother." He patted me on the back. "And just think," he said with a mischievous grin, "the weekend's only just begun."

I was so fucking screwed.

She brought a bikini with her to the lake. And not just any bikini, but a tiny red string bikini that showed off her toned, tan legs and her tight body. Her blonde hair cascaded down her back, and her blue eyes were hidden behind sunglasses that made her look like a 1950s vixen. I hadn't missed the way other men looked at her.

While I knew it was completely irrational, I wanted to rip all their eyes out. For her part, she barely acknowledged the attention, apart from a glance around here and there. But what was bothering me even more than the lecherous stares she was getting was how easy it seemed for her to not even acknowledge *me*.

I'd never been so conflicted in my entire life.

It was especially stupid since I knew exactly *why* she wasn't acknowledging me—because my daughter was sitting right next to her.

But would it be so bad if she gave me a flirty grin or something to let me know I wasn't in this torment alone and put me out of my fucking misery?

She slid her sunglasses up to sit on top of her head as she nodded to something Jenna was saying to her. As if she could feel my stare on her body, she glanced over at me while Jenna pulled a book out of her bag and immediately became immersed. Sadie's grin fell slowly and morphed into a somber expression. My relief that she was finally acknowledging me was nearly eclipsed by the defeat in her gaze. I couldn't stand it, and I ached to take away the stormy heartbreak that was brewing. I was a go-getter, a helper, a Mr. Fix-It by trade. If something needed to be done on a job, I was the one who made it happen. The same had been true since the moment I held Jenna in my arms for the first time. So, it was becoming endlessly frustrating that when it came to Sadie, I felt completely helpless about what to do.

I could confess to Jenna that I wanted to be with Sadie. She'd be mad at first, but I could probably get her to understand, right? If anyone knew how incredible Sadie was, it was her best friend.

Just then, my daughter chuckled at something she was reading and talked to Sadie, barely pulling her gaze from the page. Jenna had always been a bookworm. She was the last in her class to learn how to read and had been green with envy that the other kids could all read but she couldn't. Then once she finally figured it out, we couldn't get her to put books down. If there wasn't a book in her hand, then there was one in her purse, or on several different apps on her phone. I didn't even know how she kept track of them all, or where she found the time between her classes, her internship, and her time with friends and family.

My daughter was amazing, but she was also the only child of two people who were far too young and immature to have a child when we did. Not that we didn't do our best, and I could safely say I did everything in my power to put Jenna's needs first, but her mom didn't. Vanessa was too selfish to have a child when she did—although considering how selfish she still was, maybe her age never mattered. I'd spent Jenna's entire life trying to be the parent she could count on. The stable one who would never rip the rug out from under her like her mom always did.

My stomach soured knowing I'd turned into the very thing I had worked so hard not to be. Nothing would rip the rug out from under her more than her dad sleeping with her best friend. I'd become everything I swore I wouldn't. I always knew loving Sadie was selfish; it was easily the most selfish thing I'd ever done. But over the last week, I'd wondered if there was a way I could keep her. If there was some way to maintain my daughter's happiness as well as my own. Maybe a way I'd been too close-minded to see.

It had been a long time since I'd considered myself naive, but it suddenly seemed foolish to think I could have my own happiness without sacrificing my daughter's.

I glanced back at Sadie, and she must have seen the war going on inside me because her melancholy look mirrored my own.

She looked at Jenna and then back at me, nibbling on her gorgeous pink lip that had been in my mouth, on my cock, hell, kissed every goddamn inch of my body. I may have been ready to truly accept that we could never last, but I was nowhere near ready to be done with her.

She leaned over and murmured something to Jenna who barely glanced up from her book and nodded before diving back into it. Sadie stood gracefully from the lounge chair and pulled on her white bikini cover, slipped on her flip-flops, and then walked back toward camp. When she didn't return after five minutes, I made an excuse to go back to camp myself. No one seemed to care, but Wyatt had a smirk on his face that told me he knew exactly what I was planning to do.

Fuck him.

When I got back to camp, Sadie was sitting on the tailgate of my truck, swinging her legs back and forth like she knew I'd come for her. When she saw me, she hopped down and walked straight toward me. Each step closer made my heart beat faster with a fierce mix of lust, excitement, foreboding, and something far deeper I was still afraid to admit to myself.

"Take a walk with me," she said, and then she moved toward a trailhead nearby. She didn't wait for me to follow but she didn't have to.

I'd follow her for as long as I could.

We walked in silence for several minutes, just taking in the scenery. Our hands brushed against each other a couple of times before I gave in and clasped hers in mine, our fingers entwined together. She smiled softly toward the ground, a subtle blush staining her cheeks, and I felt my own cheeks tighten in a smile. There was something so satisfying about making her happy it almost made my chest puff up with pride.

A few more minutes passed in comfortable silence when she pulled me off the trail until we were tucked away behind some trees. In a blink, our hands were pawing at each other, and our lips clashed together like we hadn't touched in days.

"I hate this," she whispered against my mouth at the same time that she tugged at the button on my shorts.

My hands gripped her cheeks, holding her just how I wanted her so I could plunder her mouth. "I know," I said when I pulled up for breath. "I do too." Those words seemed too simple, too weak, for how torn up I was.

"I need you to make it better," she practically whimpered, and fuck if it didn't call to everything in me that was used to fixing any problem I was presented with. I knew exactly what she was asking for, and *this* was something I could give her.

Heat zinged up my spine, and my cock thickened rapidly. "Get on your knees."

She eagerly dropped to her knees, her hands already pulling down the zipper of my shorts. There was no one nearby, but even if there were, we were tucked away enough that no one would see us.

"Pull it out and suck on it," I demanded, my voice already hoarse from need.

I brushed her hair back from her face, and her eyes lit up at my demand. God, I loved her like this. She was always so eager and into whatever I asked of her. If our history together was any indication, then she was likely already soaked between her thighs. She always got turned on when I bossed her around.

She pulled out my thick cock, her soft fingers squeezing it gently—too gently for what I liked, and she knew it—before her tongue darted out and licked from base to tip on the underside while her eyes stared up at me with hunger and lust.

"Like that?" she asked, blinking up at me like a fucking innocent woman when we both knew she was a seductress.

Goddamn, she was fucking perfect.

I gripped her hair and she gasped, but her pupils flared. "Don't play with me. You know how I want you to suck it." And then I brought her mouth to my cock, and the second those perfect lips wrapped around it, she took over. She sucked my cock like she was trying to suck my heart and soul out of my body through my dick. The obscene sound of her gagging on it, sucking it deep until she could barely breathe, and then doing it all again made my legs tremble. I didn't last long—but then again, I rarely did when she was sucking me off. It felt too good and I was too needy for her. She took my cock to the hilt and I held her head against me, feeling her swallow once, then twice, and then on a low groan, I was coming in ragged bursts down her throat.

She hummed her approval as my body quivered above her and I tried to catch my breath. Leaning back against the tree right behind me, I stared down at her in wonder.

"You're fucking perfect." The words escaped before I had a chance to catch them, but I wasn't sorry. She was perfect, and she deserved to know it. Even if I could never tell her that she was perfect *for me*.

"I think I needed that as much as you did," she said, wiping my cum and her spit from her chin and the corners of her mouth.

I hauled her off the ground and kissed her hard. I used to hate when women tried to kiss me after they'd given me a blow job, but with Sadie, it felt intimate. My tongue slid into her mouth, and her whole body sagged against mine as she reciprocated my kiss.

"I haven't had my fill of you yet," I murmured against her mouth.

"We need to head back or someone will suspect."

"Not yet. Not until you come," I said as I glided my hand down her body and under her coverup. I rubbed my finger over the outside of her bikini bottoms and then moved the material aside and slid my thick digit inside her. I pulled it out and brought the finger up to my mouth, sucking on it and humming in delight as her flavor burst on my tongue.

"Oh yeah, I'm not even close to done with you yet."

I flipped us around, so she was the one leaning against the tree, and then got on my knees before her like a servant bowing down to a queen.

My queen.

I imagined what my life would be like if she really was my queen—mine to worship, to devote myself to, to give my life for. I kissed her thighs while I imagined a future that was an impossibility, and simultaneously undid the strings on her bikini until the material fell loose to the ground. I draped one of her legs over my shoulder and then feasted.

I ate her out until she came once. Then twice. I only stopped when the weight of her body sagged so heavily against me and the tree, I knew she was completely spent and couldn't hold herself up anymore.

I helped her get back to rights, and then kissed her one last time. I kissed her with everything I couldn't say, and there was such conflict in her eyes—the same conflict that was eating away at me.

We were always on the same page—it was one of the many things that made it so easy to be with her—but I could feel the pages of our chapter running out just like she could. And yet I couldn't stop myself from wanting to keep turning the pages and soaking in the warmth of her words, her body, her mind.

Rule #15

DON'T HAVE SEX OUT IN THE OPEN

SADIE

The first summer I came to the lake with Jenna, I refused to get into the water because I was terrified of drowning. If only I knew then that I'd be drowning in a different way as an adult. Instead of being pulled under by some lurking lake monster like I was always afraid of, it was Travis who pulled me so far into him I felt like I couldn't breathe unless he was near.

I had it so bad. So much worse than I ever thought it would be.

Which was probably the only explanation for why I woke up before the sun, snuck into Travis's tent, and convinced him to go watch the sunrise with me. I wondered what his excuse was for going along with it so willingly.

Whatever it was, I wasn't complaining.

We walked quietly away from camp toward the lake. There was a hush that came with being up this early when everyone else was still asleep. Once we got away from our group, Travis grabbed my hand and we walked all the way to the lake edge where Travis laid down the thick blanket he'd brought on a nearby log. We sat on it, and he wrapped another blanket around our shoulders to cut the morning chill.

That blanket had nothing on the warmth of being wrapped in his arms.

"This is nice," he said softly, as if he was trying not to disturb the peace.

"Yeah, it is," I said, snuggling closer to him. "You know, Jenna and I tried to sneak out and watch the sunrise a few times, but we always ended up falling asleep on the grass while we waited."

He chuckled. "I know. Wyatt and I would follow you to make sure you were safe and then we'd sit in our camper chairs just back there," he said, turning to point to a spot a ways away that I'd never paid much attention to before.

"Are you serious?"

He smiled down at me, and my heart galloped in my chest. How was it possible that he got even more handsome by the day? "Yeah. We thought it was cute, so we let you girls do your thing."

"I had no idea."

"You two were always off doing one thing or another. I usually gave Jenna her space, but never when her safety could be threatened. And Wyatt's always been overprotective, but that's probably what makes him so good at his job."

"Hmm," I said in response, while a million different questions passed through my mind. I wanted to ask him if he ever saw me or worried about me back then, or if it was always about Jenna, but I was afraid of the answer. Not to mention, it didn't really change anything.

"I had a crush on you back then," I admitted.

He turned to look at me, his eyes wide with surprise.

My cheeks heated as I confessed, "I saw you once, with a woman, and that's what started it, although I suppose that's not entirely true because I always thought you were handsome before that. I just didn't understand all the other things I felt until I was seventeen."

He turned back to the water, his jaw working back and forth. I could practically see the wheels turning in his head. "It was the night Jenna got in a fight with her mom and you both stayed over, wasn't it?"

"Yeah. You didn't know we were there."

He shook his head. "Not until the next morning. I'd always hoped she had no idea what happened. I always tried to keep my dating life separate and private from her unless it became something serious."

Kind of like us.

"Why didn't anything ever get serious? As long as I've known you, you've been single."

He didn't answer right away, and from the side it was hard to read his expression. "Vanessa would flaunt her boyfriends, fiancés, husbands around. Everyone knew who her flavor of the week was, and I could see how it wore on Jenna. How guarded she was with new people constantly coming into her life because they'd be leaving shortly. I didn't want to put her through that. I didn't plan to be single this long, and if I'm honest, I've dated a few women who could've been something, but when it came time to introduce them to Jenna, it never felt right, so I ended it. I always believed it'd feel right when it was the right person."

My heart cracked and my nose tingled as tears threatened in my eyes. It was what he didn't say that hit me the hardest.

I wasn't the right woman.

I knew that was the case—obviously—but hearing it out

loud hurt more than I thought it would. I wondered once again if it was worth carrying on our affair if it was only going to lead to devastating heartbreak. Why were we dragging this out when it was getting more painful by the day?

"Jenna loves you," he whispered, his voice cracking, and I glanced up at him to see him already looking at me, his own eyes a little watery and betraying how hard this was for him too. "I can't break my daughter's heart." His eyes pleaded for me to understand.

And I did.

I completely understood, even if I wished I didn't.

But understanding the why didn't make it any easier to accept. It certainly didn't convince my heart to let him go like what we had meant nothing. I already knew letting him go was going to be the hardest thing I'd ever had to do, and I was terrified that someday I might resent Jenna for it.

Which wasn't fair to her because none of this was her fault.

She didn't even know about us.

And if I was honest with myself, I'd rather my heart get broken than hers. He was right that her mom's dating history really fucked with her head. She needed the stability of her relationship with her dad. I could never live with myself if I ruined that for her.

"I hate this," I said, my voice thick with emotion and a tear escaping down my cheek.

He brushed it away and then kissed me fiercely, his tongue swiping across my bottom lip until I granted him entry into my mouth. His arm tightened around my waist, pulling me until I got his hint and straddled his lap. He cocooned us in the blanket while our lips did all the talking for us—the kind of talking that didn't need words to be understood.

I rocked against his lap, feeling him harden underneath me. Without breaking apart from our kiss, I slid my hands down and undid his pants. He lifted his hips enough to slide his pants and underwear down around his ankles, while I finagled my pants down, still refusing to break our kiss.

I sat back down on top of him, my legs straddling his, and used my hand to guide him inside me. Our lips broke apart as soon as we were joined, and we both let out soft, quiet moans that were a mix of relief, desire, and that feeling of absolute bliss. I rode him slow, my gaze locked on his, hoping he could see how much I loved him—because there was no way I could hide it in that moment.

He gripped the back of my neck and held me tighter, our foreheads resting on each other's while our gazes stayed locked and our breaths mingled.

"Sadie," he murmured.

I was afraid he was going to say something else, something I may not want to hear, so I kissed him again, refusing to let him break our kiss as I rode him, alternating between lifting up and down and grinding so my clit rubbed against his pelvis.

This was beyond reckless. We were completely exposed and out in the open, but I couldn't stop.

I didn't want to stop.

Within a few minutes, I couldn't hold back anymore and my orgasm reached its breaking point, crashing over me until bliss diffused across my whole body. I felt it in my fingertips, my stomach, my toes. Every inch of me felt this release. With one more pump he joined me, kissing me so hard, I knew my lips would look bruised and swollen for hours. I didn't know how I'd explain it, but I couldn't find the will to care.

We sat there together, breathing each other in, until the

sun started to peek over the mountaintop and the lake shimmered. This might have been reckless, but I couldn't regret this alone time with him. The quiet solitude that surrounded us while he held me in his arms like I was precious.

Like I was his.

These moments made me believe the pain that was coming would be worth it for the memories of what it felt like in his arms.

He pulled me in against his chest, and we listened as the birds chirped and the sky turned orange, then pink, then a pale blue. A contentedness I'd never felt before suffused my body. This feeling—*him*—would always be worth it, even if it broke me.

Rule #16

IF YOU WANT IT, YOU CAN HAVE IT.

TRAVIS

The sun beat down on me as I got in my truck and loosened my tie. I'd been in meetings all day negotiating prices with the rising costs of goods and meeting with architects and engineers of some of the other projects my company had going on. I also had my final meeting with Cline tomorrow where he would finally decide one way or another if he was going to sign with us, and I was nervous. It had been a long time since I'd wanted a contract as bad as I wanted this one. With the weight of everything else hanging over my head—namely Sadie—I was strung tight and on the edge of losing my goddamn mind.

I released a breath and then reached for my phone. I'd saved her name as S in my phone and now every time I saw that letter, I thought about her.

> Rough day. Go to my house and be naked when I get there.

S

Yes, sir 😉

I huffed out a laugh at her cheeky response, but as I started my truck, my shoulders were noticeably less tense, and my body was no longer tight from stress, but from excitement. It hummed in my blood, moving swiftly through my whole body. The drive home went by in a blur, and as I pulled into the garage, my blood flowed south—my cock hardening to a painful degree at the image that formed in my mind of Sadie lying naked on my bed.

Or the couch.

Or anywhere for that matter.

When I walked in the door, a red high heel greeted me and a smile lifted my cheeks. My eyes followed the trail she'd left for me—another shoe, a black pencil skirt, a red shirt. When I got to the foot of the stairs, the clothes path didn't lead up to my bedroom like I expected, but down the hall toward my office. A black lacy bra was followed by a pair of delicate black panties that had landed right in front of my office door.

I pushed it open, eager to see the woman who had me more wrapped around her finger than any other woman I'd met. The visual before me did not disappoint. Sadie was seated in my desk chair, her long smooth legs crossed at the ankle and resting on the edge of my desk while she leaned back and fiddled with one of my ties that was hanging loosely around her neck. Her vibrant blue eyes sparkled as she watched my reaction to her. A beautiful flush filled her cheeks and spread down to her chest, her full breasts perky and her nipples peaked like they were eager for what my mouth could do to them. And oh, how my mouth watered at all the filthy thoughts that filled my mind.

I wanted to do so much to her, I didn't even know where to begin.

I walked slowly toward her, my gaze never leaving hers. "Wearing a tie isn't exactly naked."

She smirked. "I'm naked everywhere else."

My gaze dropped to that sweet spot between her thighs, and even crossed, I could see moisture glistening, making my mouth water even more.

She stood smoothly from the chair and walked seductively around the desk until she was in front of it instead of behind it.

"You're stressed. Let me help with that," she said as she got down on her knees and licked her lips.

But I didn't want her mouth on my cock, at least not yet. I moved swiftly toward her and then lifted her up under her arms, eliciting a squeal as I plopped her onto my desk. My hands gripped her hips and I spread her legs wide. Her breath caught with a soft gasp that made my blood heat with lust.

"Be a good girl and grip the edge of the desk."

Her hungry gaze watched me as her hands did as I asked. My knees hit the ground, and within a breath I'd buried my face in her wet pussy. Fuck, she smelled divine—not sweet or whatever flowery bullshit some people tried to sell. She smelled like a woman—musky and even a little spicy. Every woman had their own flavor, but Sadie's was my favorite. It was the one I knew would haunt me for the rest of my days, whether we were together or not, because nothing would ever come close to how good she smelled and tasted.

I rubbed my nose up her slit, covering my face in her juices before I licked my tongue from ass to clit. Her knuckles turned white as her grip tightened on the desk and her breathing came out in staccato pants.

"This was supposed to be for you," she said, her voice shaky.

"This is for me," I murmured as my tongue slid through her juicy folds and up to that swollen little nub that elicited the sexiest noises from her mouth. She whimpered as I sucked her clit in my mouth, flicking it lightly with my tongue in the way I knew she loved.

"Oh God," she moaned, her head tipping back as one of her hands shot to my hair and clutched me tighter. I immediately stopped my ministrations, and her frantic gaze caught mine.

"Hands on the desk," I said.

She let out a mewl of frustration and need, but did as I said. The second she gripped the desk, I was back on her—my mouth licking up her flavor. I slid in two fingers, knowing she needed that internal stimulation for a stronger orgasm. The inside of her pussy was velvety soft and squeezed my finger like it was aching for something bigger. I'd give her bigger, but first I wanted to feel her explode on my tongue and squeeze my fingers with her release.

I quickened the pace of my thrusting fingers, curling them slightly with each slide out of her tight heat. She moaned on the desk, shifting like she was trying to get away from all the pleasure I was giving her, but I already had a firm grip on her thigh and there was no way I was going to let her get away.

My lips wrapped around her swollen clit, and I sucked hard at the same time that my fingers curled and slid over that fleshy bit of skin inside her. She went from trying to squirm away, to squeezing her thighs so tight against my head, holding my mouth in place as her climax wrecked her. And fuck, did it taste delicious. When her thighs eased around my ears, I lapped up every bit I could, eager to sear her flavor into my memories.

She fell back against my desk top, and she looked so incredibly beautiful laid out before me, her cheeks rosy and flushed from her orgasm, her breasts rising and falling with her rapid breaths and her legs still trembling. I stood and unbuttoned my shirt and pants, quickly stripping out of both while she watched me with hungry, sated eyes.

I wrapped a hand around the back of her neck and hauled her up until her mouth crashed against mine and I could kiss her with all the pent-up emotions of the day—and all the ones bubbling dangerously under the surface. I felt like I was on the edge of something massive, something life-altering, and her mouth—*her*—was the only thing keeping me grounded.

She moaned into my mouth, her fingers gliding over my skin, but I didn't want her gentleness. I wanted her body, her submission, her...

No.

The thought I couldn't even let my mind finish made me angry, and I roughly pulled her off the desk and then flipped her around, bending her over and sliding inside.

"Yes," she moaned as her body shook on the desk. "Fuck me. Just like that."

Fuck, why did she have to be so goddamn perfect?

I hammered into her, my anger at myself and our situation building until I was pummeling desperately inside her. With a scream, she came again, clenching so tight around my cock, I thought she might drag me with her. But fucking her from behind wasn't enough to calm the beast attempting to claw itself out of me.

Before she'd stopped spasming around my cock, I pulled

out of her and flipped her around. She was panting, her eyes heavy-lidded but still bright.

"I need more," I said, my voice ragged even to my own ears.

"Take it all," she whispered, breathless from her orgasms.

I kissed her, not rough, but not soft either. Our tongues dueled in a delicious dance, and with slightly gentler hands, I picked her up and set her back on the desk and positioned her so I could slide inside. The second my cock was fully sheathed by her tight pussy, she broke our kiss and looked at me.

My orgasm hit me out of nowhere, and with it the painful realization of what I'd been denying.

I was in love with Sadie.

Ass over head in love with her. The kind of love that nations fight wars for. The kind of love you die for. I wondered what I'd done for the universe to give me the perfect woman and make her so unattainable at the same time. But what was worse was the look that had triggered my orgasm was one filled with so much love it was breathtaking. I wanted her love. I wanted her.

For better or worse, I wanted everything I wasn't allowed to have.

Fate was cruel.

Rule #17

DON'T FALL IN LOVE WITH A WOMAN YOU CAN'T HAVE

TRAVIS

It had been a week since I'd realized I was in love with Sadie, and I'd only managed to see her a few times due to our schedules. I'd formally been offered the contract with Cline, which meant making sure things got started on the right foot so he didn't second-guess his decision. She'd also had a big project at work she was busy with. And of course, it was even harder now to be together since Jenna's internship was over. She still had a few weeks before she left for her master's program and she'd been stopping by more frequently—balancing her time between her mom and me—which wasn't exactly conducive to sneaking her best friend into my house for sex.

Although I could no longer pretend it was just sex anymore. It hadn't been for a long time. If ever.

But now that I'd admitted—to myself at least—that I was in love with Sadie, there was a new element to our encounters. Every second we'd gotten together this week—once at my office, once at her apartment—had been filled with a frantic urgency that wasn't there before. Like we both knew the end was near and neither of us were ready. We'd had more time than I thought we'd have, but I could admit the idea of letting her go was getting harder with each day that passed.

The front door opened, and I added the last touch to the food I made for our lunch. Jenna was out with her mom today, so I'd jumped at the chance to have some uninterrupted time with Sadie. To hold her, be near her, love her—even if I wouldn't say it out loud.

It seemed cruel to us both to voice something that wouldn't change where this was going.

"Travis?" Sadie's voice carried across the foyer.

"Back here in the kitchen," I called.

Her heels clacked along the floor, getting louder as she got closer, and then in another breath she rounded the corner and my heart clenched in my chest.

Fuck, she was gorgeous.

I walked around the counter, and without any words, I wrapped my arms around her and pulled her tight against my body. My mouth descended on hers, and she wrapped her arms around me, holding me close like she never wanted to let go. I continued kissing her, afraid if I stopped and spoke I might confess the very thing I swore I wouldn't say out loud to her. How much she meant to me. How much I loved her. I couldn't—not with the end looming over us.

And this had to end. Soon. Before I lost my mind and whatever shred was left of my conscience.

"I need you," she whispered urgently against my mouth before frantically kissing me again.

My hands slid down to cup her ass and I lifted her up, her legs wrapping instantly around my waist, and carried her toward my room. It was a slow journey because we couldn't stop kissing, touching, expressing our desire and need the only way we could. She rocked against me, and I nearly stumbled the last few steps to my bedroom door from the pleasure that shot up my spine.

"Fuck, Sadie."

We crashed against the wall and I let her grind against me, while I moved my mouth to kiss and suck at her neck.

"Yes," she panted.

I slid a finger under her panties and into her already slick heat. "Fuck, you're always ready for me."

"Yours," she murmured as bliss streaked across her face.

I hesitated for a second as the word hit me. Did she realize what she'd said? Did she mean it the way I wanted her to? And what if she did? It didn't change anything.

Her eyes opened and she stared at me, her gaze heavy and weighted with unspoken feelings that had been brewing since this all started. I opened my mouth to speak— to say what, I had no idea—when the front door opened and we both stiffened.

"Dad!"

"Shit," we both whispered at the same time as we separated and put ourselves back together.

"Go use the bathroom down the hall. I've been working on the downstairs one. She won't question it."

It sickened me a little with how quick I came up with that lie, and that icky feeling of deception hung over my head as I made my way downstairs without a backward glance at Sadie.

The truth was, I *couldn't* look at her. If I looked at her, I'd confess everything and blow up my whole life.

I came down the stairs and found Jenna standing at the kitchen counter looking at the spread of food. Thank God I hadn't made actual plates for Sadie and me. Now it just looked like I was making a lunch spread for multiple people.

"Hey, kiddo. I thought you'd be out with your mom for a lot longer." I walked around the counter toward the sink and washed my hands—washing Sadie off my fingers—which Jenna didn't question because I'd done this a million times before cooking or eating. That feeling of deception burrowed deeper, while also moving up to my lungs and suffocating me.

She shot me a look that said *fat fucking chance*. "I don't know why she always insists on going shopping. It's not even her money—it's her boyfriend of the month." She looked at me seriously. "Are you sure she's my mom, because the older I get the less we have in common."

I tried to hide my smile. Vanessa used to complain all the time that Jenna was more like me than her. It drove her crazy. She'd always wanted a girly girl, she claimed. What she really wanted was a daughter who was as shallow as she was. Jenna was the least shallow person I knew. She was smart and caring. She was generous with her time and was always there for her friends and family. She was the best thing I'd ever done—my greatest achievement was having raised her as a daughter.

My stomach turned at how I'd betrayed her trust.

I couldn't do it anymore.

She grabbed a baby carrot and dipped it in ranch, but before she spoke, she gestured out toward the front door. "Hey, is that Sadie's car out front?"

I opened my mouth to answer, even though I wasn't sure what to say, when Sadie came around the corner looking fresh as a daisy. "Yep. I came looking for you. Got here just a few minutes before you did and your dad said you were out with your mom. I was just using the bathroom before I was going to head out, but now that you're here, want to go out for lunch?"

Jenna looked at the spread on the counter and then up at me. "Is Uncle Wyatt coming over?"

"No, why?"

She gestured at the food. "You made a huge spread. I assumed you were expecting company."

I scratched the back of my neck. "Oh, no. I just wasn't sure when you'd be back and felt like making extras."

"Well, mind if Sadie and I join you?" She turned to Sadie. "Want to just eat here and then we can go in the pool?"

Sadie hesitated, glancing at me and then back at Jenna. "I don't have my suit."

Jenna shrugged. "That's okay. You can use one of mine."

She nibbled her lip and then gave Jenna a small smile that didn't quite reach her eyes. "Sure."

We ate around the island while Jenna filled us in on the latest email she'd gotten about her program. Sadie asked thoughtful questions and showed genuine interest while I watched the two of them. Jenna's grumpy and annoyed demeanor she had walked in with disappeared and turned into laughter the longer she talked to Sadie. I inserted comments here and there, but mostly observed.

All the while, I built up my resolve to do what I needed to do—the thing I'd been dreading.

The thing that would break my heart, but in the long run I knew it would be best for Sadie—and Jenna. Maybe mostly for Jenna, but wasn't that what a good parent did? Put their child and their needs first?

After our lunch, the girls went upstairs to Jenna's room to change and then headed out to the pool.

"I'll be in my office if you need me," I said as they walked out the back door.

Jenna turned back with a frown. "Dad, it's the weekend. You should take it off. It's not healthy to work all the time."

If only she knew how little work I'd gotten done in the last month that Sadie and I had been sneaking around—either because I'd been prioritizing time with her, or because I was distracted thinking about her. I had more than enough to get caught up on, especially now with the Cline project.

"I have a few things to finish up. I'll only work for a few hours and then I'll take the rest of the weekend off."

Her mouth twisted in a reluctant smile. "Alright."

And then she headed out, while Sadie lingered at the back door. Her expression was unreadable. Did she already know what I'd resolved to do?

I broke our gaze, looking down at the floor while I tried to build up the courage to actually do it. It was like ripping off a Band-Aid, right?

"Please, Travis," she whispered with a shaky voice, and I fought against the burn behind my eyes.

My daughter was all that mattered. Her happiness was more important than mine and we'd been reckless.

It was time to end this.

I looked up at her, my expression hard, and her bottom lip quivered before she nibbled it between her teeth.

"I'm sorry," I said, my voice strong and sure because I knew I had to be the adult here. I had to convince her this was for the best. "We always knew this had an expiration date. I think it's better if we end this now. Jenna can't ever know we did this, and if we carry on like this, we're going to get caught."

She stared at me, searching for something, then cleared

her throat. When she finally spoke, I didn't miss how hoarse her voice sounded, like she was trying to remain strong and only barely succeeding. "So that's it then?"

"Yeah. This is over."

I knew I had to be definitive, but it didn't ease the sting of the words as I watched them pierce whatever armor she thought she had up. It didn't ease how my own pain swelled in my chest. I couldn't look at her anymore—I could barely stop myself from going over there and wrapping her in my arms as it was. I wanted to comfort her, but I couldn't. I couldn't be the one to fix this.

I wasn't sure there even was a way to fix this.

I turned around and left the room, heading straight to my office and closing the door. At the last minute, I locked it. If Sadie walked through it right now, I'd cave. I was weak when it came to her—so much weaker than I should be. And if Jenna walked in, she'd know something was wrong with me and she'd dig until I confessed.

So instead, I sat at my desk and rested my head in my hands as a gaping hole in my chest grew until I felt like I couldn't even take a full breath. It had never been like this before. Not with Vanessa, not even when we divorced, although I felt like an epic failure and was devastated about not getting to see Jenna every day. Not with any of the other women in my past who I'd thought might be something serious.

No. Nothing had ever felt like the pain that was racking my body now. I couldn't concentrate on work, so I didn't even bother. Instead, I spent the next hour reminding myself of all the reasons why I had to end it.

A knock on my door pulled me out of my head, and I glanced up at it like the devil himself was on the other side.

I didn't know if I could face her yet. I knew I couldn't hide forever, but I thought I'd get a little longer than an hour.

"Yeah," I called out.

"Dad?" The handle jiggled. "Can I come in?"

I opened my laptop so at least it looked like I might've been working and then walked over to the door. When I opened it, Jenna was standing there in her sweats and tank top, her wet hair tied up in a top knot. I glanced down the hall behind her.

"Where's Sadie?"

Jenna frowned. "She left almost an hour ago. Said she got a call from her brother or something. She seemed upset, so I might go over there tonight instead of staying here."

"Okay." It was all I could say, even though I was dying to ask her for every tidbit of how Sadie had looked or what she'd said.

Jenna got up on her tiptoes and placed a kiss on my cheek. "Love you, Dad. Don't work too much tonight, okay. I'll be back in the morning."

She walked out without a backward glance, and I went back to my desk, pulled my scotch out of the bottom drawer, and poured three fingers into a highball glass.

If there was ever a time to get shit-faced and drown your sorrows, this was it.

Rule #18

NEVER FALL IN LOVE

SADIE

I was led to believe you couldn't survive without a heart, but I was proving that wrong. My heart was still sitting shattered in Travis's kitchen and had been for a week now, and it hadn't killed me yet—even if I felt like I was dying. My chest was heavy, it hurt to breathe, and I'd lost all motivation to do absolutely anything but go to work and come home. Jenna came over that night, and I managed to get her to leave without letting her see me by convincing her I was sick. It wasn't a total lie. I was so upset, I threw up because I was crying so hard. I called in sick to work on Monday, but then decided the distraction might do me some good.

It had been less than effective.

I had a new motto for life. Never fall in love; it only led to a broken heart.

My phone chimed with a text alert, but I already knew who it was. Jenna had been texting me regularly, and I knew she was worried about me, but I could barely look at her right now. Not only did I feel massively guilty about what I'd done, but I also hated that the one person I wished I could spill everything to and cry my eyes out with was her when I couldn't tell her a fucking thing.

So I ignored the text.

Unfortunately I couldn't ignore the pounding on my door fifteen minutes later. I wasn't surprised when I opened it to see Jenna's face filled with worry. One look at me and it morphed into fierce and protective.

"Whose ass am I kicking for breaking your heart?"

I thought I'd cried out all my tears, but at her question, a sob escaped and more tears came pouring out of my eyes. She walked in and pulled me into her arms.

"I'm a horrible friend," she mumbled. "I didn't even know you were seeing someone. Was it that one-night stand guy who had you all twisted up a while back?"

The tears fell harder, my entire chest heaving from my sobs. Somehow, Jenna moved me toward the couch and then pulled my head down to her lap where I cried, releasing all the emotions that had haunted me relentlessly for a week. She ran her fingers soothingly through my hair, but didn't say anything. She didn't try to make it better, and I loved her all the more for it.

Honestly, I didn't know if there was a way to make this better.

I'd never felt for anyone the way I felt for Travis.

Once the tears finally subsided and I was left with just small hiccups, she broke the silence. "What happened?" Her voice was soft and gentle, not accusing or angry that I didn't tell her when we'd never kept secrets from each other.

I sat up and grabbed a tissue from my coffee table, blowing my nose and trying to buy myself time. I adjusted so I was sitting cross-legged on the couch next to her, my gaze locked on my hands fidgeting with the throw blanket on my couch.

"It wasn't supposed to be anything serious. It was just one night, but then that one night turned into nearly every night for the past month. You were finishing your internship and dealing with your mom. I didn't want to mention it because it was just supposed to be a fling."

When I didn't continue, she said, "A fling doesn't make you cry like this. You weren't even this upset when you broke up with Greg, and you guys dated for over a year."

I nodded because I couldn't deny that she was right, but I wasn't sure what else to say about it.

So instead I went with the simple and painful truth. "I fell in love with him."

"Why didn't it work out? Did he not feel the same way?" She asked the second question like it was an impossibility, and it was *so* hard not to tell her everything. But I couldn't. I couldn't do that to Travis. Jenna was his whole world.

"No, he didn't." The words scraped on their way out. Fresh tears filled my eyes, and my nose burned from the effort of holding them back.

"Oh Sadie, I'm so sorry." She pulled me tight against her. "For what it's worth, he's obviously an idiot if he can't see how incredible you are."

I cried harder because if she knew who it was, she'd hate me instead of sitting here consoling me while I tried to figure out how to live with a broken heart.

"You need something to take your mind off this," she said.

"I'm not having sex with someone else."

She rolled her eyes. "That's not what I was going to suggest. There's a little get-together going on tonight. Low-key, but would be a good excuse to get out of your apartment. What do you think?"

It was probably a good idea to get out and try to function in public instead of just at work. Low-key sounded like low-pressure which meant if I wanted to leave, I could. Jenna had never led me wrong before, and I knew if I decided it was too much, she wouldn't be bothered if I left.

"I'll drive," she said before I had a chance to say anything. "You go get changed, I'll do your hair, and I'll get some ice to bring down the puffiness of your eyes and then we'll head out, okay?"

"Okay," I said, swallowing down the emotion lodged in my throat and reminding myself that I would get through this.

Somehow.

I should've asked for more details.

When we pulled up outside Travis's house, I glanced at her. "Did you need to pick something up?"

She looked at me funny. "No. The party is here. Uncle Wyatt convinced my dad to throw a barbecue thing. I figured this would be a safe bet since it's all people who love you and no pressure. You've practically grown up in this house."

She got out of the car so fast she couldn't see my face blanch. I turned to look out the window at the house where I had my heart broken.

The house that no longer held warmth and happy feelings, but pain and heartache.

She came around to my side and looked in the window at me, arching a brow. I took a deep breath, hoping it would give me strength—already knowing it wouldn't—and then got out of the car.

"We don't have to stay long. Maybe just eat a burger, listen to Uncle Wyatt's corny jokes even though we all know he's got all the exits mapped out and is probably the most dangerous guy in there, and then we can go back to your place, eat some ice cream, drink something alcoholic, and watch movies until we pass out."

"Maybe we should just skip to that last part at my place," I mumbled as we headed toward the gate that led to the backyard. I could already hear voices, lots of voices. It had been a while since I'd been to one of Travis's backyard parties, and I really wished I wasn't walking into this one. I wasn't prepared to see him.

We walked into the backyard to find small groups of people mingling, Wyatt at the grill, and a few people already in the pool. Laughter filled the air. Obviously, Travis hadn't been struggling like I had. He was throwing a fucking party only a week after obliterating my heart. If I needed any confirmation that my feelings were one-sided, this was it.

A knot formed in my stomach which only grew when I spotted Travis with his friend Troy, who also worked with him. Troy's wife, who I'd met at past barbecues, stood next to a petite brunette who was looking at Travis like he was a juicy steak.

"Hey Dad," Jenna said, grabbing Travis's attention, which shifted to me at the same time Jenna asked, "Who's this?"

Travis opened his mouth to speak, but Troy was the one who answered.

"This is your dad's hot date for the night," he said with laughter in his voice, and that knot in my stomach was suddenly nothing compared to the way all the air whooshed out of my body at his declaration.

My gaze finally broke away from Travis to look at Troy, who seemed proud of himself. Then I glanced at the brunette, and whatever semblance of my heart that was left splintered and crumbled in my chest. She looked closer to Travis's age and was petite and beautiful in every way.

She was the exact opposite of me.

I didn't think it was possible to feel any lower than I had in the past week, but realization dawned as I felt like every piece of me broke inch by inch. This was the kind of woman he wanted—older, more sophisticated, and the kind of woman he would be able to show off to his friends and introduce to his daughter.

He never wanted me—he was never going to be mine, no matter how badly I wanted it.

If I stood there for another second, I was going to break in front of everyone and there would be no way to hide that reaction. And right now, Travis was the last person who I wanted to see me break.

"Excuse me. I need to use the bathroom."

I moved toward the house while the conversation continued behind me, but instead of heading toward the bathroom, I pulled out my phone and called for an Uber. I walked straight through the foyer and out to the front yard. In two minutes, a stranger picked me up and took me home where I fell apart in the privacy of my own space, determined to never let Travis know how much he'd broken me.

I'd never be so stupid as to fall in love ever again.

Rule #19

NEVER LET YOUR FRIEND SET YOU UP WITHOUT YOUR PERMISSION

TRAVIS

Shit shit shit.

That was all that kept going through my head as I watched Sadie walk into the house after Troy opened his big, stupid mouth about the blind date I didn't fucking want or ask for. All because he thought I was moping too much at work this week.

I gritted my teeth, my jaw clenching painfully as I tried not to be obvious about constantly glancing back at the house waiting for Sadie to re-emerge. I needed to see her face and know that she was okay.

My chest ached and my stomach pitched painfully as I recalled the look of complete and utter heartbreak on her face when she looked at the woman Troy brought for me. I needed to find a way to clear up the situation. I couldn't stand the idea of her thinking I'd moved on so quickly like she was meaningless to me when that couldn't be further from the truth. I'd been a shell of a man without her. I'd never been so fucking miserable in my entire life.

Fuck, just the few minutes I got to see her was like getting air after being deprived for too long. She looked so beautiful it almost hurt to look at her. Although, that wasn't entirely true. She looked tired. And her eyes drooped in the corners in a way I hadn't ever seen before.

She looked as sad as I felt. And I hated that I couldn't take away her hurt. I hated even more that I was the one who hurt her.

And then her sadness morphed to even greater heartbreak as she'd looked at my "date," and I couldn't bear the idea of her hurting so much over a complete misunderstanding.

I caught Jenna glancing at the house as well, a deep furrow between her eyebrows and a frown on her face. I sidestepped closer to her—and farther away from my too handsy "date"—and bent down, lowering my voice so only she could hear me. "Is she okay?"

Jenna barely spared me a glance before her gaze was back on the house. "I don't think so." She nibbled her lip, but never moved her gaze from the house. Then she confided, "She's heartbroken over some guy. I've never seen her like this before, and I'm really worried about her. I thought getting out of her apartment might do her some good, but she was hesitant as soon as we got here. Maybe I pushed too soon."

I felt sick. Completely and utterly sick to my stomach with a heavy dose of guilt. I didn't know if I felt more guilty for what I'd done to Sadie or for putting my daughter through all this concern over her friend.

Or for lying. I was definitely feeling guilty over the giant lie hanging over my head.

"I'm going to go inside and check on her," Jenna said and then immediately headed into the house. A few minutes later she came back out with her head bent, her eyes focused on her phone in her hand and that frown still firmly in place.

"Everything okay?" I asked, walking toward her without even bothering to excuse myself from my group. I knew I was being a terrible host, but I couldn't find it in me to give a shit.

Jenna shook her head and looked up at me. "She left."

"What?"

She glanced back at her phone and I could see her reading a text. "Yeah, she said she wasn't feeling good." She said it like she knew it was a lie, and that knot in my stomach tightened.

"Are you going to go over there?" She usually did—it was what they'd always done for each other—and I needed to know Sadie wasn't alone and in pain. I needed someone there since I couldn't be.

But Jenna shook her head. "No, she said she needed space tonight. I don't know who the hell this guy is, but he really fucked her up."

I already felt like shit for what I did to Sadie, but hearing Jenna's scathing remark delivered with such anger and venom felt like I'd been ripped in half with a sword covered in acid. Despite my insides feeling like they'd shriveled up, I kept my face neutral.

"I think I'm going to head to my own place and check on her in the morning. I'm not feeling very social anymore."

I dropped a kiss to her head. "Okay. Drive safe."

"I will." She stepped away from me and threw a wave to Wyatt at the grill, who frowned when he realized she was leaving already, and then she exited out the side gate where she'd entered barely thirty minutes ago. I watched after her until she was out of sight, and when I turned around, Wyatt was almost to me.

"She's leaving already? Wasn't Sadie with her?" I must not have kept my face as composed as I'd hoped because his gaze softened with sympathy. "Oh fuck. You ended things, didn't you?"

I tried to clear my throat to speak, but couldn't, so I just nodded.

"When?"

"A week ago," I said, my voice hoarse.

"So you weren't antisocial this week because you were busy with Sadie; you were avoiding everyone because you were without her."

I nodded.

"Does Jenna know?"

I shook my head, but then added, feeling like I needed to justify my decision, "She almost caught us together. It was too close. We were playing with fire, and it was better if we ended it when we did."

He scrutinizes me. "For whom?"

"What?"

"Who was it better for? Because from where I'm standing, you look like shit and are clearly miserable. The fact Sadie was here for a hot second before splitting suggests she's not doing well with it either. So who exactly was it better for?"

He knew. He had to know, so I didn't understand why he was going to make me say it.

"I don't have time for this," I mumbled.

"Cut the shit, Trav. Who was it better for? I want to hear you say it."

"Jenna, okay? It was best for Jenna. Is that what you want to hear?"

"See, now here's where I'm noticing a fatal flaw. Jenna just walked out of here with a huge frown on her face, but she didn't seem pissed at you, so I'm gonna assume she's worried about Sadie. So how is that better for her? Did you ever consider just telling her about you and Sadie?"

My eyes bulged, and anger and helpless desperation ripped through me. "Are you fucking kidding me? What would that accomplish? She'd never be okay with it."

"How do you know?"

"Because it's not appropriate. I'm her dad and Sadie is her best friend who's twenty fucking years younger than I am."

"So it's the age gap that's bothering you?"

I slammed my fingers in my hair and looked up to the sky. "I'm not doing this with you right now."

That helpless desperation clawed at me until I felt like something was crawling beneath my skin. I had to get out of here.

"You're in charge of this," I said, and then fast walked into the house, swiped my keys and wallet, and got into my truck.

I was pulling up to Sadie's apartment building before I even realized it.

I ran up the stairs, two at a time, and then pounded on her door. I heard feet shuffle toward the door but she didn't open up. My forehead rested on the door while my hands braced on the doorframe, and my eyes closed with how close and yet how far away she felt from me.

"I know you're in there. Open up, Sadie. Please," my voice broke on the last word, and maybe that worked in my favor because she opened the door, and my stomach immediately plummeted. Her eyes were red and puffy and filled with the same devastation I'd felt all fucking week.

Wyatt's question circled my brain. *Who was it better for?*

We were both in pain and miserable without each other. None of this felt right, but I didn't know how to have her and not lose my daughter.

She wrapped her arms around herself, so closed off from me, and I hated it with every ounce of my being.

"Sadie," I whispered, my voice broken and my eyes burning with the threat of my own tears.

A sob ripped from her throat, and I couldn't take the distance anymore. I stepped forward and wrapped her in my arms as she crumbled against me, soaking my shirt with her tears. I held her tight, shuffling us all the way into her apartment so I could kick the door closed. I dropped kisses to the top of her head, held her tight, and whispered whatever I could think of to soothe her.

Nothing seemed to help.

I swept her up into my arms and moved us to the couch, sitting with her on my lap, but still holding her close as she cried. With every sob and hiccup, she ripped my heart to shreds.

"I'm so sorry, Sadie," I said, my voice hoarse and ragged. "It wasn't what it looked like. It was a blind date. I didn't ask to be set up. Troy thought I needed cheering up because I'd been a mopey bastard all week. I've been fucking miserable without you. I can't stand to see you hurting," I added, whispering against her hair.

She sat up and her eyes were a little clearer. Then her gaze dropped to my mouth, and the tension that had been between us since that first night flared thicker than ever.

"Can...can I have one more kiss?"

I shook my head even as my face moved incrementally

closer to hers. "It's not a good idea," I whispered, just a breath away now.

Her hungry eyes moved from my lips to meet my gaze. "It's only a kiss," she whispered.

"No, it's not. It never was," I said right before I gripped the back of her neck and hauled her mouth to mine, releasing a week's worth of longing into our kiss.

For weeks I'd asked myself how I was going to survive this woman when all this time I should've been asking myself how the hell I thought I would survive *without* her. The guilt that ate away at my insides when we were together was nothing compared to how torn up I was when we were apart.

Like it always did, the kiss escalated until her shaking fingers loosened the buttons of my shirt while my hands slid underneath her baggy sweatshirt to squeeze her full breasts that were blessedly unrestrained by a bra.

The fewer clothes to get in my way, the better.

Our mouths melded together like they were made for each other, our tongues completing a dance we'd perfected in our time together.

Fuck, she made me feel alive.

Our clothes were in disarray, our hands everywhere as our lips refused to part when a knock sounded at the door. She pulled back, dazed, with her lips swollen from our kiss. Another knock and we both glanced at the door before she slid off my lap and went to open it while I attempted to redo the buttons of my shirt.

I didn't know if it was her distraction from my words or our kiss, but she didn't look through the peephole before she swung the door open. In the hall stood Jenna who smiled softly at Sadie and held up a bottle of gin. "I was going to give you space, but then I..."

Jenna's gaze slid to me still sitting frozen on the couch, and her soft smile morphed to confusion. "Dad? What are you doing here?"

But even as she said the words, her confusion cleared to understanding, shock, and maybe even a little disgust when she took in my disheveled appearance along with Sadie's obviously red and swollen lips. There was no way to hide what we had been doing. I stood, ready to speak, but I was at a complete loss for words.

Her gaze shot to Sadie. "My dad? My fucking *dad* is the guy who broke your heart?"

Sadie shook her head—not in denial but almost as if she wished there was some way to stop the train wreck I could clearly see coming. "Jenna—"

Jenna held her hand up. "No. No. You don't get to say another thing right now. I...I need some time to wrap my head around this." She handed Sadie the gin, shot me a death glare, then walked away.

I was torn between running after her and staying to fix things with Sadie, but when Sadie turned around, her arms were crossed and her body language was completely guarded. Her eyes were now clear and angry, which I supposed was easier to take than her heartbreak.

"Please go. We have nothing left to discuss." Her voice was devoid of emotion.

"Sadie—" I said, stepping toward her, but she held up a hand to stop me just like Jenna did to her.

"No. You made it clear where we stood and what you wanted a week ago. I get it now. You were right. Now I want you to leave."

She didn't get it at all, but my head was so fucked-up—over her and now Jenna finding out—that I didn't know how to explain what I really wanted. I didn't know how to tell her that I was in love with her and could barely breathe without her.

I didn't even think she'd hear me because I'd never seen her so closed off.

What the fuck had I done?

I thought being caught would blow up my whole life. Turned out, letting her go was all it took to light the dynamite.

My shoulders fell and I walked out the door, which Sadie slammed shut as soon as I exited. I ran my hands through my short hair.

I needed to talk to Jenna.

Rule #20

THE TRUTH WILL SET YOU FREE

SADIE

The bright California sun, chirping birds, and distant sounds of laughter were so at odds with the feelings roiling inside of me as I stared at my best friend on the patio of our favorite coffee shop.

"Thanks for meeting with me," I said, my hands cupping my coffee.

Jenna nodded, but still sat with her arms crossed, the coffee I bought her sitting untouched on the table.

"You wanted to talk. So talk."

"I'm sorry," I said, my shoulders sagging.

I texted Jenna last night after Travis left, and after I realized she wasn't going to answer any of my dozen phone calls. She agreed to meet with me, and I knew I had a lot of damage control to do.

"I never should've done it," I whispered.

It was hard to say those words because I didn't regret my time with Travis, even as heartbroken as I felt now and even though I was sitting across from my best friend with no certainty that she even wanted that title anymore. But it was also not a lie to say I shouldn't have been with him, because I knew from the start that this was the likely outcome.

Her brow furrowed and jaw shifted back and forth like she was chewing on her words. "Have you guys been going behind my back for years?"

"No!" I leaned forward, my whole body emphasizing the word. "No, it was recent. About a month or so ago, I saw him at that masquerade ball for the Los Angeles Historical Society and then ran into him again a few days later. Do you remember when I was supposed to have a date with that Josh guy I met on the dating app?"

She nodded.

"Well, he couldn't make it—something about getting called into an important surgery or something. But Travis—your dad," I corrected. "He was there with a potential client and stopped at my table on his way out. When he found out I got stood up, he joined me so I wouldn't have to eat alone. It was..." I covered my mouth with the tips of my fingers and fought back the surge of emotion the memory brought up. It was the best date I'd ever had, but I doubted she wanted to hear that. I shook my head and changed gears. "That's when it started. It was only going to be the one time, but, well, then it wasn't."

She leaned forward, her gaze now slightly more curious than guarded. "What were you going to say before? It was...what?"

"It doesn't matter," I said, staring down at my coffee instead of her. She could read me too well, and she was clearly persistent because she didn't give up.

"It does matter, and you used to tell me everything."

The hurt in her voice fed the guilt already eating away at me, so I closed my eyes and confessed. "It was the best night of my life—everything about it. The date. The way he made me laugh. The way he made me feel. His touch. It was by far the best date I've ever had. We clicked like I never have with anyone else. And after..."

"Okay, I changed my mind. You don't need to go into those details. I just wanted to know about the date. I don't want to know about the *after*."

"Fair enough."

She picked up her coffee and finally took a sip before placing it back on the table. "Are you in love with him?"

"I think the answer to that is pretty obvious by now," I said, my voice small, smaller than I'd like.

"I want to hear you say it, I guess."

Emotion choked me, but I swallowed it down and met her eyes. "Yes. I'm in love with him."

She watched me carefully. "So, then what happened?"

How could I tell her the truth? That *she* happened. That we were doomed from the start because neither of us wanted to hurt her and knew it would never work.

I shrugged and told her another truth I'd come to terms with. "He didn't love me, and it ran its course."

Her eyes turned to slits. "I saw you two last night, not to mention the last week. He's been miserable. So have you."

I shrugged again. "I don't know what you want me to tell you, Jenna. He ended it, but the truth is we both knew there was an expiration date. It's my fault I let my heart get involved. I should've known better."

Silence descended between us, and neither of us spoke for several minutes.

"Were you two together at the lake?"

"Yes," I admitted.

She looked off to the side and nodded. Then her gaze shot to mine. "That day I came by his house after shopping with my mom—you weren't there to see me, were you? You'd been there with him?"

This one was harder to admit because it brought up memories of everything that happened after she showed up. "Yes."

Sympathy and understanding filled her eyes. "That's when he ended it, wasn't it?" she asked, her voice now soft. "That's why you left suddenly."

I nodded.

She sat back in her chair and shook her head. "I can't believe I didn't see it."

"You were busy with your internship for most of it."

She was still staring vacantly to the side, and I could practically see her replaying the last month in her head with this new information.

"Do you hate me?" I whispered. I had to ask. I had to know where I stood with her. I'd already lost Travis. I didn't think I could stand losing her too.

Her attention focused on me, and she shook her head sadly. "I could never hate you. I'm mad that you guys kept me in the dark, and personally I think it's a little gross cause he's my dad. But,"—she cocked her head back and forth—"I can also kind of see it. You two have a lot of the same interests. You've never had good experiences with guys our age, so it makes sense that you'd click with an older guy. Despite the fact that he clearly broke your heart, I'd say he's a good guy and you deserve one of those. So, no, I don't hate you. I'm still not entirely sure how I feel about everything, though. I'm gonna need a little more time to process it all. I think what bothers me the most is that you lied about it."

"I know. I'm so sorry. I just...I've liked him for so long and I knew you'd never approve. I guess I just wanted what I knew I wasn't supposed to have."

She stared at me, her eyes holding a mixture of emotions —sadness, hurt, confusion—but she didn't correct my assumption that she wouldn't be okay with it. Even now, I knew she wasn't okay with it.

"Am I going to lose you? Because I don't think I can lose you too." My voice broke and a tear slipped freely down my cheek. She leaned forward, putting her hand out palm up on the table, and I immediately grabbed it with mine.

"You're not going to lose me. You're stuck with me for life, remember? Ride or die, to the grave."

I gave her a watery nod, and we sat in the silence for a while. She occasionally asked questions while we finished our coffee, but she could see how much I was hurting, so she asked about other things like work, or if my brother's fiancée could get us tickets to an LA Wolves game since she was one of the coaches.

Eventually, we parted ways with a tight hug, and I could breathe a little easier knowing I still had her. My heart was broken, but the world didn't end.

I could move on from this.

Maybe if I kept saying it, I'd believe it.

On my way home, I stopped by the store to pick up some groceries because it was time to pull myself together as best I could and get back to normal—whatever that was now —and my kitchen cabinets were painfully bare. I was standing in front of the avocados, wondering if they were worth the purchase or if they'd ripen and go bad before I ever had a chance to eat them, when a male voice from beside me pulled my attention up.

"Sadie?"

My mouth gaped in surprise. "Josh. Hey." It felt like so much had happened since the night he stood me up.

He smiled and he was just as handsome as I remembered from his pictures, but he didn't make my whole body light up like Travis did. There was no flutter in my chest or tightening of my stomach from desire.

"I thought that was you. You're way more beautiful than your pictures, and you were already stunningly gorgeous in those." He kept his gaze focused on my face like he couldn't look away to save his life. "My schedule has lightened up with this new rotation I'm on. I'd love to take you out for real sometime and cash in that rain check. I know you blew me off when I texted you after that night, but I'd really like to make it up to you."

I nibbled my lip, unsure. I was still nursing a broken heart, but maybe this was for the best. I couldn't be with Travis, so there was no point in holding on to a dream that would only ever be just that—a dream. Josh wasn't going to be the love of my life, but he could get me out of the house and serve as a distraction for a few hours.

There were worse reasons to go out with an attractive doctor.

So I agreed, even as the thought of going on a date with anyone besides Travis felt like a betrayal. "Sure. I'd like that."

"Are you free tomorrow night? There's a great restaurant in Beverly Hills I've been dying to try. I'd love to take you."

I nodded and we finalized the details. As much as my insides protested the date, I reminded myself that this was for the best.

I needed to be realistic, and it was time to let Travis go.

Once and for all.

Rule #21

DON'T TRY TO FIGURE OUT YOUR LIFE WHILE DRUNK

TRAVIS

I was staring at the drink in front of me when I heard the front door slam. If it was a robber, they picked a good night. I didn't have the energy to move, let alone defend my house. Maybe they'd put me out of my fucking misery.

I tossed back the finger of whiskey and then grabbed the bottle to pour another when my office door swung open. Jenna stood there with her hands on her hips, scoping out the scene before her. I didn't think I'd ever looked this bad in front of her before. I always made sure to keep my shit together—although I was never nursing a broken heart either, so it wasn't hard to maintain a certain sense of decorum.

"No offense, Dad, but you look like shit."

I huffed out a laugh and then took another drink. I couldn't even look at her. The guilt was bad enough as it was, but if I actually had to look at her, I didn't think I'd ever be able to face myself in the mirror again.

"What's wrong with you?" Her voice was soft and her tone concerned, which didn't jibe with how accusatory her words were. It took my muddled—read drunk—brain a minute to register that she was asking out of concern, not scorn or anger.

So I took a chance and glanced up at her. Her soft brown hair that was the same shade as her mom's hung loosely to her shoulders, and her eyes were filled with so much sadness it gutted me. I did that. I put that look on her face. Twenty-two years with a great record as a dad and I went and tore it all to hell.

For a woman.

For the perfect woman. The woman of my goddamn dreams, who was so off-limits it wasn't even fucking funny.

I threw back the rest of my drink, wondering how long it'd take to kill all the brain cells that remembered the feel of Sadie. Remembered how light I felt when she was around. Remembered her laugh and the way she'd hold my hand, her fingers soft and without calluses, so unlike mine.

I wasn't sure there was enough alcohol in the world to burn away all those memories.

"Dad?"

"Hmm?" I glanced up at her and realized she was saying something that I'd clearly missed.

She squinted at the bottle of whiskey on my desk. "How drunk are you?"

"Not drunk enough," I mumbled, grabbing the neck of the bottle to pour another glass, but she yanked it out of my hand and put it on the shelf behind her where I couldn't reach it.

"Not tonight, Jenna," I said, my voice worn and weary. "Can we do this tomorrow? You can yell and scream at me and call me a pervert then. It's nothing I haven't said to myself a million times anyway. I just...I just can't tonight. Okay?"

"Answer one question for me and I'll go."

Sagging back in my chair, I let out a heavy sigh. "Fine. What?"

"Do you love her?"

I clenched my jaw and glanced at the bottle of whiskey that I needed in order to drown out the rush of emotion that overcame me with her question. Any question but that one.

"I can't answer that question," I gritted out.

"Why not?"

I shook my head.

"Why not, Dad?"

"Because I never even told her!" I shouted as I stood from my seat, my temper short and my heart a goddamn mess.

Jenna's eyes filled with tears, and I felt like the worst scum of the earth. What was happening to me?

I fell back to my seat and put my head in my hands. "Please just go, Jenna. We'll talk tomorrow, but I can't do this tonight."

"You're an idiot, you know that?"

I glanced up at her, and she had her arms crossed and looked royally pissed off. I knew that look. It was the one she always wore whenever she was about to dig her heels in. Her stubborn streak could be a mile long—something she inherited from me.

"I'm taking your whiskey. Sober the fuck up, Dad. We'll talk in the morning." She spun on her heels and then walked toward the door, but before she exited she turned back to me. "I'm staying here tonight, and in the morning we're talking about Sadie. She deserves better than this, Dad."

I blinked twice, sure I'd heard her wrong, and she turned to leave. "Wait," I said, standing up but having to brace myself against the desk when I started to wobble. "What do you mean by that?" The words came out slower than usual and a little slurred, but still clear enough to be understood.

"You said you didn't want to talk about it." Her gaze turned skeptical as she looked me up and down. "And frankly, I don't think you're in any condition to have a serious conversation. You smell like you took a bath in a distillery."

"What did you mean about Sadie not deserving this?"

That one sentence from her had given me an ounce of hope I was terrified to hold on to overnight. I needed her to clarify so I could properly prepare myself for the verbal lashing she was going to give me tomorrow.

Her gaze softened and she sighed with exasperation. "You're the best Dad, you know that, don't you?"

I shook my head—hesitant and subtle. I didn't feel like a good dad at all.

"No, I suppose you probably wouldn't think that right now. And despite your recent actions, you're not usually a giant jackass. Sadie deserves a man who fights for her, one who will love her out in the open. She doesn't deserve to be treated like a dirty little secret."

"It wasn't like that," I was quick to say.

She arched her brow. "Wasn't it?"

Shit. Okay, so it was, but it also very much wasn't. Sadie never felt like a dirty little secret. I was never ashamed of her. If anything she felt like a dream, one I kept to myself because she was never supposed to be mine.

But fuck, she felt like mine.

She must've seen the turmoil on my face. "We'll talk tomorrow. Take an aspirin and get some sleep."

With another blink, she was gone and I was left with my thoughts...and a small kernel of hope.

Our morning talk turned into an early dinner talk because Vanessa called Jenna with an "emergency" in the morning which turned out to be her latest fiancé calling off the wedding. I suspected she already had someone else lined up, but she needed Jenna to come over and comfort her because she was apparently devastated.

Sometimes I wondered what I'd seen in Vanessa. We couldn't be more different if we tried, but I also couldn't regret our time together because it gave us Jenna, and I wouldn't trade her for the world.

"Dad! I'm back," Jenna called as she came through the house.

"In the kitchen," I hollered, and she walked in to find me making her favorite—Philly cheesesteaks. She came around the island and gave me a kiss on the cheek before resting her head on my shoulder. The affection made my heart squeeze. She'd always done this, and I was worried I might've lost it with how I'd behaved lately.

"How was your day?" I asked her, tilting my head to rest on hers.

She let out a little sigh. "Mom was...Mom. You know how she is, especially after a breakup."

I did, and I'd watched Jenna deal with it more times than she should. My guilt over Sadie came roaring back.

Jenna moved over to sit on one of the stools. "Anyway, thanks for making dinner. Are you ready to talk?"

"Do I have a choice?" I asked as I put the meat and melted cheese into the sandwich buns and placed them on plates.

"Nope."

She let me get situated at my own seat before she gave me an impatient stare. I took a bite of my sandwich, hoping to buy myself some time, and then washed it down with some Coke before finally leaning forward and resting my elbows on the counter. "I'm sorry, Jenna. That's really all that I can say. I'm sorry."

"For what exactly?"

I glanced over at her, confused by her question. "What do you mean?"

She watched me carefully. "Are you sorry you hooked up with her? Or because I found out the way I did? Or are you sorry because you fell in love with her?"

"I..." My throat went dry and I stared at her, not sure what to say. "I'm definitely sorry you found out the way you did. I should've known better than to get involved with her."

She frowned. "So you regret being with her?"

My heart stuttered. No. That was the clear answer, but I knew that wouldn't be easy for Jenna to hear. Was there any harm in laying it all out on the table now?

"No, I don't regret being with her."

"I asked you a question last night and you alluded to an answer, but you were also drunk, so I'm going to ask you again. Are you in love with Sadie?"

I looked back down at my plate of food, but my appetite was gone. "It doesn't really matter, does it? It's over. We never should've gotten involved as it was. It wasn't fair to you."

"What the hell do I have to do with your relationships?"

I stared at her, dumbfounded. "That's a joke, right? She's your best friend! She's way too young for me. There are a million reasons we shouldn't be together."

"Age gap romances aren't that taboo anymore, Dad. There are a ton of romance novels written with that trope every year, so that's not a good reason not to be together. And the other reason—"

"The part where she's your best friend—"

"Yeah, that one. Is that what's holding you back? If I gave you my blessing, would you be honest with me about what you want with Sadie?"

"Is that what you really want? Honesty?"

"I thought I'd made that pretty clear," she said.

My jaw clenched, but I no longer hesitated. "Then here's the truth. I've never met another woman who made me feel anything close to what Sadie made me feel for her. Do I love her? Yes. Yes, okay? I'm in love with her. I can't stop thinking about her and I hate—*hate*—knowing that I broke her heart because I'd rather rip my own to shreds than ever hurt hers. I'd rather suffer than ever cause her suffering. She's fucking perfect. Completely, utterly, fucking perfect and I'm so in love with her it hurts to breathe without her. Is that really what you wanted to hear?"

My heart was pounding and my whole body ached from the confession I'd been holding back for so long, but then she reacted in a way I never would've expected.

She smiled, her eyes holding more knowledge than I'd ever given her credit for. "Yeah, that's exactly what I wanted to know."

I felt like I'd been socked in the stomach and I was waiting to get my air back. This had to be a horrible trap of some kind.

"Dad, I'm not gonna lie. It's a little weird—okay, really weird—because I've always viewed Sadie as a sister, and it's strange to think of you two *together*, but just because it's strange doesn't mean I can't get used to it. You're the two most important people in my life, and my favorite people in the world. If you make each other happy, who am I to stand in the way of love? It's probably going to feel weird for a while, and I'd appreciate if you kept the PDA to a minimum in front of me until I adjust, but I want you two to be happy. You're both clearly miserable apart, and I don't want either of you to come to resent me because you felt like I got in the way of your happiness."

I grabbed her hand. "I could never resent you, Jenna. You're the most important thing in the world to me."

"I know, Dad. And I appreciate that you've always put me first, but I think it's time you did something for yourself. And I think you need to be honest about what you want."

I knew what I wanted. I'd known since the moment I ended things and nothing in my life felt right anymore.

"I want Sadie back."

Jenna smiled wide. "Good. Then let's figure out how you're going to win her back." She pulled out her phone.

"What are you doing?"

"I'm texting her to see if she's home," she said, never looking up from her phone. "She probably is since she's..." Her mouth parted and she sucked in a breath.

"What? Is she okay?"

She looked up at me and there was an apology in her suddenly hesitant gaze.

"She's on a date."

My entire body stiffened. "No, the fuck she is not."

Sadie was mine. I just needed to convince her to give

me a second chance. "Find out where she is. I'm not waiting any longer than I already have to tell her how I feel."

Jenna's worry morphed to thrill, her smile wide and her eyes taking on that hint of mischief she always got when she was hatching a plan. "I was hoping you'd say that."

Rule #22

YOU GOTTA LEAVE WITH THE MAN YOU CAME WITH

SADIE

I stared down at Jenna's text again, but she hadn't responded again since I'd told her the Cliff Notes version of my date so far. I tucked my phone back in the pocket of my dress and grabbed my wine as Josh came back from the bathroom. Ever since she texted me asking where I was, I'd wondered if I should be hanging out with her instead of on this date. This horrible, horrible date.

"Sorry again about the change of location. I should've known the other restaurant would need reservations, but at least now it's like a real do-over," he said with a bright smile as he adjusted his napkin on his lap.

Yes, a do-over in the same restaurant he stood me up in.

The same restaurant where everything started with Travis—at least where he knew who he was actually flirting with.

I chugged another large mouthful of wine.

This night might've been easier to get through if Josh and I had any sort of chemistry, but we'd been here for over half an hour and I'd felt all thirty of those minutes with painful slowness. He was a nice guy, but there was no spark, not even a tiny flicker. And being here in this restaurant with the absence of a spark only made me feel even more hollow because I knew what I was missing.

The way Travis's eyes watched me with an acute awareness during our dinner. How we laughed easily, talked easily, simply enjoyed each other easily.

Maybe that was where it went wrong. It was too easy. That should've been a red flag. Relationships are never easy. They're hard work. They take constant effort. Or at least that's how mine have always been. I thought the fact that everything was different with Travis was a good thing. Like maybe we could find a way to make it work.

Now I just felt naive and pitiful.

"Sadie?"

"Hmm?" I pulled my gaze up from the crisp white tablecloth where it had wandered and then subsequently zoned out.

"You okay? You seem distracted."

God, I was being a horrible date. "I'm sorry, Josh. It's not you, I promise."

He sat back in his chair watching me. He really was handsome with his stereotypical California blond-haired, blue-eyed surfer physique, and I had no doubt he'd make some lucky woman very happy someday. It just wouldn't be me.

"The old 'it's not you, it's me' line. I haven't heard that one in a while. Do you want to talk about it?"

I shook my head and then looked out the window, not wanting him to see the hurt I couldn't hide in my eyes. "There's nothing to talk about."

"I'm not so sure about that," he said, but it sounded

mumbled. I could feel the presence of another person and I assumed it was the waiter, but then *his* scent hit me, and I had to close my eyes against the pain that suffocated me from the smell.

Travis's cologne.

I'd know it anywhere.

I pulled myself together the best I could and turned my head, and even though I knew it was his scent, the fact Travis was actually standing here, next to my table while I was on a date with another man, made my mouth part and my eyes stare in complete disbelief.

What was he doing here?

His gaze was filled with so much love—wait, no. Not love. It couldn't be love because he'd made it clear he didn't feel that way, but it was the look I'd always thought meant he might love me, and now I felt stupid all over again.

"Travis." I glanced behind him. "Are you here for another work meeting?" I was proud of myself for how composed my voice sounded.

"I'm here for you."

I gaped at him in shock, but quickly pulled myself together. "W-what?"

His gaze was fierce and locked on mine. "You can't date this guy."

"Excuse me?" Josh said at the same time I said, "Why the hell not?"

Travis bent down, placing both his hands on the sides of my chair, trapping me with his body, and oh God, I wasn't strong enough to be this close to him and not completely fall apart.

"Because you belong with me, the same way I belong with you."

I must've heard him wrong, or had too much to drink,

although I only had the one glass of wine. "You don't want me." My words were barely a whisper, but it felt like they ripped my heart a little more as they escaped into the air.

He shook his head slowly, his hazel gaze never leaving mine. "That's not even close to true. I'm fucking miserable without you. I love you so much, Sadie, it hurts to breathe without you next to me."

I didn't even realize that silent tears had slipped down my cheeks until he brushed one away with his thumb, and my voice was noticeably thicker when I whispered, "You don't mean it."

He couldn't. We both knew why we couldn't be together. I didn't know why he was saying this now when it didn't make a damn bit of difference. "I don't know why you're trying to hurt me—"

He cut me off, his own eyes shining with pain and regret. "The last thing I want to do is hurt you again. I'm not bullshitting you. I'm in love with you and I don't want anyone else. You're it for me, Sadie."

"What about Jenna?"

He leaned closer, as if he needed to be nearer to me. "I already talked to her and told her how I feel and that I need you." I inhaled sharply, not expecting that at all.

"She gave me her blessing. How'd you think I knew where to find you?"

I hadn't thought that far. My brain had been a mess since the second I caught his scent. It didn't even cross my mind to ask how he knew where I was, but what he said made sense.

"You need me?" I asked him, afraid to hope.

He squatted down so we were now face-to-face. "More than I could ever express with words. You are the light of my life, the air I breathe. You are everything. Please, Sadie, give me another chance."

Another tear slipped down my cheek as I threw my arms around him and kissed him with everything I had.

I followed Travis back to his house, and the second my car was in park, I pulled the keys out of the ignition and jumped out of the car. He'd done the same, and we met in a clash of bodies, our lips melding and our groans morphing together until I couldn't tell who was making what noise.

It felt so good to be in his arms again. So right.

I broke our kiss, my chest panting. "We should go inside so someone doesn't see."

He peppered my jaw and neck with kisses. "Let them see. Let the whole world see that you're mine." He pulled back. "We're not hiding anymore, Sadie. I'm never hiding how I feel for you again."

I didn't think my heart could be filled with any more joy if I tried.

"No more hiding," I whispered as happy tears filled my eyes. His gaze softened into something tender, and that look of love was there again, so strong, so sure, that the only thing I could do to express all this crazy big love inside of me was to throw my arms around his shoulders and kiss him hard.

His hands cupped my head, holding me to his mouth as he took over the kiss in the way I loved so much—dominant, possessive, hungry. He slid his hands down and lifted me up into his arms, carrying me into the house like a groom carried his bride.

And I wondered if someday I'd really get to be his bride.

My lips tilted into a smile even as his kiss deepened because I knew I would. This was it.

He was it for me.

The big love I'd always craved. The man who would love me as fiercely as I loved him.

He carried me up the stairs all the way to his room and then placed me gently on the bed.

"I love you," he murmured as he stripped me of my clothes and kissed his way down my body. "I love your laugh, your smile, your intelligence, your humor, your body. I love it all."

I would never tire of hearing him tell me he loved me.

He knelt between my legs and then stared up at me as he kissed each thigh, teasing me before his talented tongue licked up my pussy to my clit.

"Travis," I breathed.

His eyes turned dark and hooded. "You're mine, Sadie."

"Yes," I whispered, and then immediately fought back a moan as he flicked that glorious tongue against my clit before sucking it into his mouth. Tremors racked my body, and one of my hands gripped his hair, holding him to me as my body shook.

"And I'm yours," he said as he slid one of his thick fingers inside me, easing his way through my already slick cunt.

"God, yes," I moaned.

He pulled his finger out and then slid a second one inside and curled them every time he pulled out, rubbing on a spot that made me see stars. His mouth descended back to my clit, and he alternated between sucking and thrusting his fingers until my orgasm exploded through me.

"Fuck, you taste good," he said as he continued to lick

me through my release and caused little tremors to spike through me.

He kissed his way back up my body until he reached my mouth and kissed me deep, parting my lips with his tongue and allowing me to taste myself. His hands ran gently up and down my sides until I placed my palms on his chest and pushed him to his back, rolling over and straddling his waist. He smiled up at me, and my heart surged with happiness at his carefree joy. I did that. I put that look on this gorgeous man's face. I made him happy.

This couldn't be real.

"I love you," I told him, and his hungry, happy gaze turned tender with love—the same look I always doubted before, but would never doubt again. I leaned down and kissed him, loving how his hands instantly slid in my hair. My mouth moved over his chiseled jaw, then down his neck. I kissed down his chest, nibbling his nipples and loving the sharp inhale I got from him when I did. I made my way down his stomach, trailing kisses, licks, and nibbles until I reached the edge of his pants. I slid off the bed and removed his shoes, then undid his pants and wiggled them off, pulling his underwear down with them and leaving him gloriously naked on the bed. His hot gaze never left my face as I got him naked and then climbed back on the bed until I was resting between his legs. My fingers gripped his stiff erection, loving the velvet feel, even as I admired how incredibly hard he was just from going down on me.

"This is mine," I said, glancing up at him.

He nodded and when he spoke, his voice was ragged. "Yours."

My gaze never left his as I bent over and took him in my mouth, sliding my tongue on the underside of his cock, along the thick vein there. I pulled off and swirled my tongue along the head, then licked the bead of precum before sucking just the tip of his cock like it was the best tasting sucker I'd ever had in my mouth.

"Goddamn it, Sadie," he groaned, barely holding himself together. His entire body was stiff with restraint, his muscles bulging and his chest moving in shallow breaths. I loved it when he got like this. When I made him like this.

He moved his hand through my hair, his molten hazel gaze watching my every move. "Suck that cock. That's my good girl. So fucking good," he groaned.

My pussy clenched as I felt moisture pool there. I loved it when he talked dirty. Doing as requested, I sucked the head of his cock hard until he groaned again.

"Fuck yeah. Just like that." He pushed my head down a bit. "Take it all, baby."

Before he had even finished his demand, I took him to the back of my throat and swallowed, focusing on breathing through my nose so I could hold him there.

"Oh God, yes. Right there, baby. Oh fuck, Sadie, you're gonna make me come."

I moaned as I pulled my mouth off his cock, swirling my tongue around the tip and then taking him all the way again. This time he held my head there as he practically lifted his upper body off the bed and released a guttural groan. My eyes watered as my clit throbbed almost painfully between my thighs.

"Enough," he growled, gently pulling my head off his cock and flipping us over so he was on top. He kissed me fiercely. "Fuck, what you do to me, woman. But I don't want to come down your throat—not tonight. I want to come in this perfect pussy," he said as he slid his fingers inside me, eliciting another moan from me.

"Fuck, you're so wet for me. You like sucking my cock."

"I love it," I said, staring at him boldly. His mouth tilted into a cocky grin and then he kissed me again until we were both breathing heavily and more worked up than before.

He notched his thick erection against my pussy lips and then slid in. I was so wet, it was an easy glide, but he was big enough that he still stretched me, and we both inhaled sharply at the exquisite ecstasy of being connected so intimately.

He moved inside me with perfect strokes because he knew my body. He was the only man I'd ever been with who had taken the time to learn every inch of me and what made me feel good.

He whispered naughty things in my ear as he thrust in and out until my climax crashed through my body and I screamed his name. With two more deep pumps, he came inside me and then collapsed on top of me. His heavy weight felt so good after the aching hollowness of missing him this past week, but it was nothing compared to when he wrapped me up in his arms and we fell asleep—peaceful, content, and completely together.

I'd never been more certain that this was where I belonged.

Rule #23

DON'T LEAVE THE PARTY WHEN YOU'RE THE GUEST OF HONOR

TRAVIS

THREE YEARS LATER

My wife held our nine-month-old son in her arms, a smile wide on her beautiful face as she talked to Jenna. I had offered to take Hunter, our son, off her hands, but he was a mama's boy through and through. I watched her, my heart feeling fuller than I'd ever known was possible.

She'd been wandering around the party for the last hour, making sure she talked to everyone who came to celebrate her twenty-fifth birthday—from friends and family, to even a few business associates we had in common. Walter Cline was among them with his wife by his side. Sadie had won him over the first time I introduced them, and it was another reminder of how stupid I'd been to ever worry about what he might think of my relationship with her. As it turned out, he thought I was a very lucky man. We were in agreement on that fact.

Some days my life seemed surreal—like it couldn't be this easy to have everything I wanted. It didn't seem normal to be this happy all the time. To be this satisfied with life. But then again, most people didn't have a woman like Sadie in their life. I still remembered all too clearly how empty my life was before her, and I was thankful every day that she gave me another chance after I pushed her away.

I was thankful for Jenna, too, for accepting us, even if I knew it was hard for her at first. I worried maybe she hadn't meant it when she gave me her blessing to be with Sadie, but she had assured me many times over the years that she did, that she had never seen Sadie so happy. When she stood at Sadie's side at our wedding two years ago, I finally believed her.

It was just another piece that added to my endless happiness.

Unable to stay away from my wife—I'd never tire of calling her that—any longer, I moved to her side, wrapping my arm around her waist as I dropped a kiss to her head and moved my other hand to our son's back. She looked up at me with her bright, gorgeous smile that never failed to leave me a little winded.

"This was such a great surprise," she said.

I nodded at Jenna. "It was all her idea."

"Well, I love it. Thank you both for putting this together," she said as she leaned against me.

Jenna smiled wide. "Anytime. Now hand that baby over. I have crazy baby fever, and he's just too stinking cute for my sanity."

We both laughed as Jenna stole Hunter from Sadie's arms and then proceeded to make silly faces until he broke out in giggles.

She'd just given me the opening I was looking for. "Actually, Jenna. Would you watch him for a bit?"

"Sure thing. Just don't get caught," she said with a singsong voice, her gaze never leaving the baby's.

Sadie buried her face in my chest, but her shoulders shook with laughter. Sadie made me insatiable, even after three years, and unfortunately, we'd been walked in on or overheard a couple of times—once by Wyatt, and once by Jenna's fiancé.

Without waiting to be further teased by my daughter, I grabbed Sadie's hand and dragged her into the house. We ended up in my home office because it was closer than our bedroom and I couldn't wait to have her. The door was barely closed before I had her pushed against it, my hands diving under her dress and straight into her panties. She moaned as my fingers glided smoothly through her already wet folds.

"Fuck, I've needed this all goddamn day."

"We had sex this m-morning," she stuttered as I brushed across her swollen clit with my thumb while I slid two fingers inside her.

"It's not enough," I said as I nibbled her ear and then down her neck. "Haven't you figured out by now that it's never enough? I'm always going to want more of you."

She let out a contented sigh and then pulled my face up until our mouths brushed against each other. "Good. I like you addicted to me."

I growled and dove in, taking our kiss deeper while my hand thrust mercilessly inside her pussy. I could already feel her tightening around my fingers, so close to coming. Instead of letting her tip over the edge, I pulled my fingers out, causing her to let out a whimper in frustration.

"Don't worry. You'll come soon enough. Be a good girl and pull your panties to the side," I said as I quickly undid my pants, shoved them down, and then positioned myself at her now exposed entrance. I slid home in one easy thrust.

God fucking damnit, the feel of her was unreal—even now. She'd been nervous that having a baby would change our sex life, which it did to an extent because it wasn't always easy to find time to have sex, but it sure as hell hadn't changed my desire for her or how fucking good she felt wrapped around my hard cock.

"Fuck, Trav," she moaned, her hips alternating between rocking and grinding, seeking out her pleasure. Her head was tilted back against the door and her eyes closed.

"Look at me," I demanded as I continued to relentlessly pound into her. Her eyes popped open and her gaze connected with mine. Heat stirred deep in my belly as I stared into the eyes of the love of my life, my wife, my heart and soul. This woman was everything I'd ever hoped to have in a partner and so much more.

She rocked faster, her eyes heavy-lidded and her breathing labored. Her arms wrapped tighter around my neck while her thighs squeezed my hips. She was right on the edge. I reached into the tight space between us and rubbed her clit with my finger to give her the friction I knew she needed while I thrust deep inside of her with my cock. She cried out as her orgasm broke through her and then clamped so tightly around me there was no way to stop my own orgasm from barreling through me.

She sagged in my arms, and I braced one hand against the door to hold us up. I dropped my head to her shoulder and sucked in a deep inhale, getting a hit of her perfume mixed with that familiar scent of our sex.

"I love you so much," I murmured.

Her arms tightened around my neck as she replied, her voice light and relaxed. "I love you too. Thank you for building this amazing life with me. I feel incredibly spoiled, and not just because it's my birthday."

I pulled back enough to look her in the eyes—her beautiful blue eyes that were filled with happiness and love. This woman never ceased to amaze me. "I'm the one who should be thanking you. You give me and everyone around you so much. It's only fair we return the favor and show our appreciation. Me especially." I laid my forehead on hers. "You've given me the whole world, Sadie. I'd be nothing without you, at least nothing that mattered. You deserve everything and more."

"I just want you...and maybe one more kiss before we go back out there."

I narrowed my gaze at her, which caused her to laugh—the sound light and carefree.

"What?" she said. "It's only a kiss."

Bonus Rule

YOU CAN'T HAVE BATHROOM SEX AFTER YOU HAVE KIDS.

SADIE

"Oh fuck."

My fingers gripped his hair, tugging on the strands he'd let grow out the last few weeks. His strong hands held my thighs down as he continued to devour my pussy. My legs shook as my orgasm got closer.

"Travis. Oh God, I'm close."

He growled but didn't slow his pace. My muscles tightened as his magical tongue took me higher and higher until stars exploded across my vision, my back arched, and my body convulsed in an orgasm so intense I thought I'd died and been brought back to life.

He licked me through my release, slowly bringing me back to earth.

"Goddamn this pussy tastes amazing," he practically growled against my wet folds.

I brushed my fingers through his hair, watching him with wonder. His gaze locked on mine and he didn't look away as he moved slowly up my body like a predator watching his prey.

When he was only a breath away from my face, I slid my hands through his hair once more before cupping his face and bringing his lips to mine.

"It's yours," I whispered against his lips before they connected.

He hummed in agreement and deepened the kiss. His tongue licked across the seam of my lips and I granted him entry—I'd never deny him.

We'd been married for ten years and some days I couldn't believe how lucky we were.

Someone banged on the bathroom door. "Please tell me you two are not getting it on in there!"

We pulled apart and burst into a fit of laughter. Travis stepped back, readjusting the obviously hard length straining against his jeans. "To be finished at home."

I sat up on the countertop, no longer leaning against the mirror, and hopped down, pulled up my underwear, and fixed my skirt.

When I spun around to check my hair in the reflection and make sure I was all put together, Travis came up against my back, wrapping his arms around me.

"Have I mentioned lately that I love all these skirts you wear."

I smirked. "You've mentioned it a time or two." Or twenty. It was why I wore them.

Travis opened the bathroom door for me and I walked out to find Jenna leaning against the wall directly across from the door, her arms crossed.

"You two have a problem," she said, shaking her head like she was massively disappointed in us. I arched a brow and reveled in the blush that stained her cheeks at the unspoken reminder that I caught her and her husband doing the same thing last night.

"Whatever," she said, fighting back a grin. "I covered for you. Addie was looking for you, but Ford took her to play with him and Hunter on the beach."

"Who's watching them?" Travis asked suddenly on alert. No one was more protective of our kids than this papa bear.

"I was until I came in here to get you two. Now my hubs is hanging out with them, but we have plans tonight, so you two need to knock it off or Addie won't be the baby for much longer."

I didn't tell her that Travis got a vasectomy after Addie was born. We both decided three kids was enough and didn't want to take any risks. But there were still some things I didn't share with my bestie given that my husband was her dad.

We came up to Big Sur to spend the long weekend at the vacation house Jenna's husband bought here. They found time to get away every month or two, but we hadn't been able to come here in over a year.

"Connor's out there with them," she added when Travis looked like he was about to come out of his skin with worry that the kids were near the water unsupervised. That eased his tension. He'd come to love Connor, even if he wasn't sure about their relationship when they first started dating.

"Come on, babe. Let's go find our kids." I smiled at Jenna and then grabbed my husband's hand and led him outside. We went down the stairs that led to the beach and found our three kids building a sand castle with Jenna's husband.

Our oldest, Hunter, had a serious furrow to his brow as he tried to get the sand to mold exactly the way he wanted it. At seven years old, he was the most serious of our children. Ford, our middle child, was five and I was genuinely amazed he was sitting still long enough to even attempt a sand structure. He had endless energy and rarely stayed in one spot for long. Our three-year-old daughter, Addie—short for Addison—glanced up from where she was sitting in Connor's lap. A huge smile broke out on her face and then she was pushing out of his lap and racing toward us.

"Mommy!" she squealed.

I let go of Travis's hand and bent down just in time to catch her in my arms.

"Hey, sweet girl. Are you keeping your brothers in line?"

She leaned back in my arms and nodded once. "Yep," she added, popping the P.

She was a mama's girl through and through and I loved it. Hunter was a mama's boy up until he turned two and then he wanted to be just like his daddy. Ford has always marched to his own beat.

Addie burrowed into my hold, wrapping her little arms tightly around my neck and I squeezed her tight.

Travis watched me with that smile—the one that was just mine, filled with wonder and love. I reached out and he took my hand, giving it a squeeze before he pulled me and our daughter into his side.

"Thank you," he whispered into my ear.

"For what?"

He pulled back and his gaze traced every line of my face. He brushed a stray strand of hair away from my eyes. "For giving me the life I never thought I'd have. For being an incredible and loving wife and mother. You never cease to amaze me."

Addie wiggled in my arms and we both chuckled as I

put her down and watched her race back to her brothers and Connor.

Leaning my head against my husband's shoulder, I whispered back. "Thank you for being the best husband and partner a girl could hope for." I wrapped my arms around his waist and watched his eyes darken with love and lust. "You are my dream come true."

I loved this man, and the life we'd built together. I loved that even after ten years together he could still bring me the greatest pleasure I'd ever known followed by the most tender and heartwarming moments like this one.

As I curled into my husband's side and watched our children play on the beach, I sent a silent thank you to the universe. No matter what challenges may come, I knew the man at my side would always love and support me through it all.

How lucky was I?

Want early access to future releases? Join Cadence's Crew, an exclusive reader community for fans of Cadence Keys. Interested? Check out https://reamstories.com/cadencekeys to learn more.

ACKNOWLEDGMENTS

I wrote this book as a palate cleanser after the heaviness of my rockstar series in November 2022. It was meant to be short and steamy (okay, let's be real. I wanted ALL THE SMUT.) and I think I succeeded.

This book was a ton of fun to write, but after I wrote it, I honestly wasn't sure if I was even going to publish it or not. It wasn't really like anything else I'd written before and it was much more sex driven than character driven (although some of that worked its way in there because I can't help myself). I held onto it for a long time, unsure if I should really give it to my editors, or if I should just put it aside and chalk it up to a fun writing experiment that would never see the light of day.

And then I decided to say "fuck it" and publish it anyway. I'm happy to report I have zero regrets about it. I love the feedback I've gotten, but more importantly I love these characters, and I'm really happy that now their story is out in the world for other people to love as well.

Like all my books, I wouldn't have been able to write or publish this book if it wasn't for the amazing team of people in my corner.

First and foremost to my husband, for his endless love and support. He tells everyone he meets that his wife writes romance (literally everyone, including his doctor and nurses at a recent appointment he had) and I couldn't be more thankful for him. He's my hype guy and the person who makes my writing time possible.

To my kids, L & A, thank you for giving me purpose. I love you more than you could ever know (but I'll sure as hell try to show you every day).

To my editors, Ann Suhs and Ann Riza. I would be so lost without you both. Thank you for always helping me make my books shine!

To Lily Bear Designs for the GORGEOUS special edition cover.

To my beta readers for giving me priceless feedback on how I could take my story to the next level.

To all my loyal readers who have purchased this book and read it even though it's not like any of my others. Thank you for your endless support. Thank you doesn't feel like enough. You've helped me achieve my dream life and my gratitude for you all is endless.

And to all my new readers who just found me through this book. Thank you for taking a chance on a new to you author. I hope you'll stick around :)

ABOUT THE AUTHOR

Cadence Keys is a bestselling steamy romance author. When she's not coming up with plots for her books, she's chasing her rambunctious toddlers around or cuddling with her husband. She loves writing heartfelt stories with relatable characters and a guaranteed happily ever after.

Learn more about her and her books on her website: www.cadencekeysauthor.com

facebook.com/cadencekeysauthor

twitter.com/cadencewrites

instagram.com/cadencekeysauthor

bookbub.com/profile/cadence-keys

goodreads.com/cadencekeysauthor

ALSO BY CADENCE KEYS

LA Wolves Football Series

In the Grasp

Across the Middle

Down by Contact

Taking the Handoff

Defending the Backfield

After the Snap

Rapturous Intent Rockstar Series

Noble Intent

Forbidden Intent

Devoted Intent

Promised Intent

Breaking the Rules Series

Only a Kiss

Just for Tonight

www.ingramcontent.com/pod-product-compliance
Lightning Source LLC
Chambersburg PA
CBHW031751200726
48289CB00013B/786